This book belongs to

....

A Story a DAY

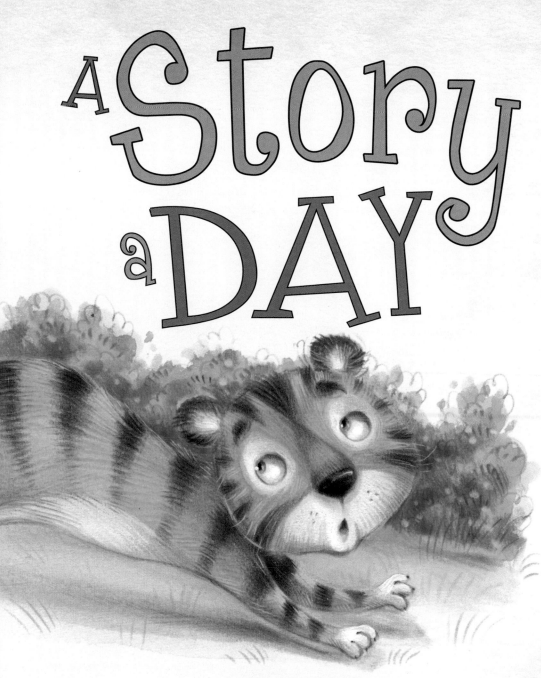

Compiled by Tig Thomas

Miles Kelly

First published in 2015 by Miles Kelly Publishing Ltd
Harding's Barn, Bardfield End Green, Thaxted, Essex, CM6 3PX, UK

2 4 6 8 10 9 7 5 3 1

Publishing Director Belinda Gallagher
Creative Director Jo Cowan
Editorial Director Rosie Neave
Senior Editor Claire Philip
Design Manager Simon Lee
Production Elizabeth Collins, Caroline Kelly
Reprographics Stephan Davis, Jennifer Cozens, Thom Allaway

ISBN 978-1-78209-811-9

Printed in China

British Library Cataloguing-in-Publication Data
A catalogue record for this book is available from the British Library

ACKNOWLEDGEMENTS

The publishers would like to thank the following artists who have contributed to this book:

Cover: Kelly Caswell (Advocate Art), Sharon Harmer (The Bright Agency)

Frank Endersby
Advocate Art: Claire Keay, Christine Battuz, Jon Davis,
Sarah Lawrence, Hannah Wood, Ela Jarzabek, Sophie Burrows

All other artwork from the Miles Kelly Artwork Bank

Made with paper from a sustainable forest

www.mileskelly.net
info@mileskelly.net

Foreword

Discover a story for every day of the year! In this collection there are stories to make you smile and stories to make you think. You'll find funny stories, silly stories, fairytales, fables, legends, myths and folk tales from around the world. They are all short enough to be read in less than ten minutes – perfect for a burst of imagination and wonder. Enjoy a year's worth of storytelling in a single book – what story will you read today?

JANUARY

The Sunflower

There was once a sea nymph with long golden hair called Clytie. She wore beautiful green gowns woven of seaweed and lived in the very depths of the ocean. One day, she heard a mermaid singing a song about the golden light hanging in the sky, and she longed to see it.

Clytie swam to the water's surface and climbed onto the shore. There she saw the sun for the first time! It was so beautiful that she stood gazing at it all day long.

As night fell she looked down into the water at her reflection. Her golden hair had become yellow petals, her green gown was made of leaves and her tiny feet had become roots. She had become a sunflower!

And to this very day, all sunflowers turn on their stems so that they can gaze upon the sun as it travels across the sky.

The Giant who Counted Carrots

High upon a mountainside lived a giant. He spent his days growing carrots, and was very lonely. One day, he was out walking when he came across a group of young women near a rock pool. They were sitting with their toes dangling in the water and laughing happily.

The giant hid and as he watched from afar, he fell in love with one, whose name was Elizabeth. When they eventually skipped away, the giant felt sad. He decided he would try to win the girl's heart. He lined the rock pool with silver, and filled it with golden fish. Then the giant hid away again and waited for them to return.

When the girls came back they were astonished. Elizabeth looked deep into the silver pool and heard

a voice telling her to step into the water. As soon as she did so, she found herself in the giant's garden.

He begged her to stay with him and be his queen, but she told him she loved a duke, and that they were engaged. The giant hoped Elizabeth would change her mind, but she soon grew pale and sad. In the hope of cheering her, the giant gave her his magic staff. Anything it touched would turn into an animal.

He also took Elizabeth out into the fields to show her his carrots. Elizabeth asked the giant how many he grew, but he couldn't tell her. However she begged him to count, and as he began she quickly drew out the magic staff, and touched a black stone. At once it turned into a black horse, and Elizabeth mounted its back and fled down the valley.

The next day, Elizabeth married her duke. The giant was so sad and lonely that he fell into a deep sleep. In time, grass grew all over him until he was completely covered. Locals named the mound 'Giant Mountain', and it is still called that today.

The Moon-cake

A little boy was just about to take a bite out of his cake when a bigger boy said, "That cake would be much prettier if it was shaped like the moon."

The little boy liked the sound of that.

"I can make it look just like the moon," promised the big boy, with a grin.

"Really?" asked the little boy. He cautiously handed over his cake over to the big boy, who at once took an enormous bite! The cake was now shaped like a crescent-moon.

"No!" cried the little boy.

The big boy urged, "Don't worry — I'll neaten it into a half-moon for you."

And he nibbled off the horns of the crescent. But when the little boy saw that, he began to wail. The big boy then explained that just before the new moon comes, the old moon disappears. So he swallowed the rest and ran off!

The Snowman

A snowman watched, unblinking, as the sun went down one evening. As he gazed, the moon rose, large, round, clear and beautiful in the dark blue sky.

"Here it comes again," said the snowman, thinking that the moon was the sun coming back. "I hope it gets light again soon so that I can see myself. Even more, I'd love to be able to run about."

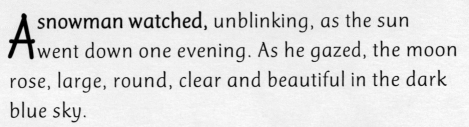

"Woof!" barked a dog, who was playing nearby. "The sun will soon teach you to run. All snowmen end up running away!"

"I don't understand," the snowman answered.

Then a young couple came walking up to the snowman. "Isn't the snow wonderful?" the girl exclaimed. "Even summer isn't as beautiful as this."

"Who were they?" the snowman asked the dog, after the couple had walked away.

"They are our masters," answered the dog. "They let me sleep by the stove — look, you can see it through that window over there."

The snowman shuffled over to the window and peered through. "How beautiful the stove looks!" he cried. "I wish I could get in there and be close to it!"

The next day the sun rose high in the sky and shone even hotter than the day before, but the snowman didn't mind, or even notice. All he could think of was the stove.

Little by little he began to drip and melt away, and soon there was nothing left of the snowman except a a hat, a rake and a carrot, lying together where the snowman had stood.

The Fox, the Rooster and the Dog

One night, a fox was prowling about when he saw a rooster perched nearby. The fox quickly thought of a plan, and cried, "Good news!"

"What is it?" asked the rooster.

"King Lion has declared that all the animals should live in peace," declared the fox. "From now on, no beast may hurt another."

"Why, that is good news," said the rooster, "and I see someone with whom we can share it."

"Who is it you see?" said the fox.

"My master's dog is coming to meet us," the rooster said but the fox began to run away.

"Will you not stop and tell the dog the good news also?" called the rooster.

"I would," muttered the fox, "but I fear he may not have heard of King Lion's new law."

You can't fool everyone.

The Rabbit's Bride

There was once a woman who lived with her daughter in a cottage. They had a large vegetable patch where they grew delicious cabbages, but one day a large rabbit hopped into their garden and began to eat them.

The daughter ran out crying, "Shoo!"

To her surprise, the rabbit spoke to her. "My dear," it said, "come and live with me in my underground burrow."

"Certainly not!" said the girl. The rabbit just shrugged and leapt away.

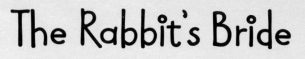

The next day, the rabbit was back. Once again the girl ran out crying, "Shoo! Don't you dare eat up all our cabbages!"

"I won't," said the rabbit, "if you come and live with me in my burrow!"

Suddenly, the girl had an idea. "I will," she said. She put on her coat and hat and hopped onto the rabbit's tail, and he bounded away. When they reached the burrow, the rabbit said, "Now, get to work and prepare a feast. I am going to invite my family to the wedding."

As soon as the rabbit had gone, the girl took some straw and tied it with twine to make a figure about the same size as herself. She dressed it in her coat and hat and painted a face on it. Then she ran all the way home to her mother.

After a while the rabbit returned. "Hello," he said, "how are you getting on?" But as he touched the figure its head fell off and rolled away!

"Oh my!" gasped the rabbit. "I've killed her!"

And he scampered away, as fast as he could leap, promising never to touch cabbages again!

The Fisherman Piping

A fisherman once had a great idea for a new way to catch fish. He thought that if he took his flute to the riverbank and played a jolly tune, the fish might hear the music, and come to the surface and dance. Then the fisherman could catch them easily.

So he began to play one merry song after another, but not a single fish put so much as its nose out of the water. The fisherman gave up, laid down his flute, and went back to his old method of just casting his net into the water.

To his astonishment, when he drew the net in it was heavy with fish! Then the fisherman took up his flute and played again, and as he played, the fish flipped and flapped in the net.

"Ah, you dance now when I play," said he.

"Yes," replied an old fish, "now that we have no choice."

When you are in a person's power you must do as they wish.

The Wolf and the Seven Little Kids

Mother goat had to go to market, so as she was leaving she told her seven little kids, "Do not let anyone into the house until I return."

A wolf saw her leave, and knocked on the door. "Open up! It's your mother, back from her trip—"

"No!" said the little kids. "Mother has a soft voice."

The wolf ate some honey to soften his voice, then he put his black paws up to the window and asked to be let in. "No!" said the kids, "Mother has white feet!

So the wolf covered his feet in flour, and this time the kids opened the door. One by one he ate them all up! When mother goat came home she found only one remaining – for he had hidden inside the grandfather clock! Then mother goat went and found the wolf, and kicked him so hard that the other kids flew out of his mouth. The wolf fled, and was never seen again.

The Boy who Cried Wolf

There was once a shepherd boy who often got lonely and bored out on the hillside, so one day he thought of a plan to amuse himself. He rushed towards his village shouting, "Wolf! Wolf!"

The villagers came running to help him but when they realized there was no wolf, they went home grumbling. A few days later the naughty boy tried the same trick and again the villagers came rushing to help him. They were very angry, however, when they realized they had been tricked a second time.

Just a few days later, a wolf really did begin prowling around the sheep. Of course the boy set off crying, "Wolf! Wolf!"

But the villagers thought that the boy was lying again, so nobody came to his aid and the wolf ate the boy's whole flock.

Liars never prosper.

The Tall Story

Five blind men were sitting by a road one morning when they sensed something near them. The first man put out his hand and felt something rough and solid. "It's a wall!" he said.

One

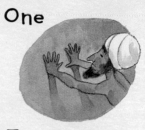

The second man reached out. "No, it's a spear," he said.

Two

The third man felt too. "No, don't be silly, it's a piece of rope."

The fourth man stretched out and wrapped two arms around something, "No, it's definitely a tree trunk."

Three

And the fifth man argued, "You are all wrong, I can feel a snake."

A boy nearby laughed at them all. "You're all silly. It's an ELEPHANT!"

Four

The first man stopped touching the elephant's side, the second man let go of his tusk, the third man dropped the tail, the fourth man stepped away from the leg, and the fifth man took his hands off the trunk. And they never quarrelled again.

Five

The Little Matchgirl

It was winter and in the biting cold a poor little girl was walking barefoot through the streets.

In her ragged old apron she carried bundles of matches. She had been trying to sell them all day, but no one had bought anything.

In all the windows of the houses around her, lights were shining — all the families were celebrating New Year's Eve with big roast dinners. When the little girl reached a sheltered corner formed by two houses, she sank down, exhausted. She dared not go home — her father would be angry that she hadn't sold any matches.

The little girl blew on her hands to try to bring them back to life. Then she thought that if she lit a match, it might give her warmth.

She drew one out and struck it firmly against the wall. It gave out a bright flame, like a little candle, and when she held her hands over it, the match was warm and wonderful. It flared up, and when the light fell upon the bricks, it was as if they became transparent and she could see inside the house.

There was a table on which a roast goose steamed away gloriously on a big platter! But then the match went out.

The little matchgirl hurried to light another match. Suddenly, she was sitting under a beautiful Christmas tree. The girl stretched out her hand to touch it ... but the match went out.

'Just one more,' the little matchgirl decided, and in the brightness stood her grandmother.

"Grandmother!" cried the child. "I want to stay with you!"

Her grandmother came to the little girl and held her in her arms. Then she flew away with her in the brightness up to heaven, where there was neither hunger nor cold, only joy.

The Lambkin and the Little Fish

Long ago, a cruel woman hatched a plan to get rid of her stepchildren. She was a witch so one day she whispered a spell and pfff! her little boy turned into a fish! The witch dropped him into the castle moat. Then… pfff! she turned the little girl turned into a lamb. The very next day, the witch ordered her cook to kill the lamb for dinner. The cook went to the meadow to carry out the task, but at the last moment the lamb cried out, "I will always love you," to her brother, the fish, who was swimming nearby in the moat.

The cook realized that the animals were actually the children, and he rescued them both. He took them to live with an old wise woman, who undid the spell and kept them with her in the forest. She taught them good magic — and the children lived with her very happily for many years.

The Farmer and his Dog

One day a farmer was hard at work in his field, mending a gap in one of his fences. He had left his young child asleep in a cradle nearby, thinking that the baby would be safe. But when he returned he found the cradle turned upside down! The bedding was torn, and his dog was covered with blood. The farmer thought the dog had attacked the child, so he furiously chased it away.

But when he turned the cradle over, he found his baby unhurt, and soon noticed an enormous snake lying dead on the floor – killed by his faithful dog. The farmer called the dog back, washed its wounds and cared for it kindly for the rest of his life.

The Six Swans

Years ago, a king married a witch's daughter. She was beautiful but had a mean heart.

Now, the king had seven children – six boys and a girl – who he loved dearly. He didn't tell his new wife about them, however, as he knew she would be terribly jealous. He kept his children a secret for a while, but his wife soon found out about them. She decided to get rid of the children and made some enchanted white shirts, one of which she threw over each boy.

Instantly, they became swans and flew away! But the little girl ran away and hid in the forest. The next morning, the girl decided she had to do something to save her brothers, so she packed her bag and went out to seek them. She travelled all day, and was just about to settle down for the night when six swans flew down and transformed back into her brothers!

"Oh my goodness!" she cried, "It's you! Isn't there any way I can break the spell?"

"Yes," they said. "But it is a hard task. For six years you must go without speaking or laughing. And you must sew six shirts made of white flowers."

The girl agreed at once, and the very next morning she began to sew. She did not speak to anyone, as her brothers had instructed.

As she worked, a king came riding by. He fell instantly in love with the girl and asked her to marry him. She nodded, and even though she remained silent they were very happy together. Months and years passed and still she didn't speak. Every day she sewed the shirts, trying to get them just right.

Eventually she gave birth to a baby, but one night, the king's mother stole their son away. She didn't trust the girl and thought that her silence was witchcraft. Then she told her son that his queen had killed their child! The king did not believe his mother but his advisors insisted that the laws of the land be followed. And of course the queen could not speak to defend herself! Luckily, however, she had finished all six shirts, so she took them with her as she was brought out for her punishment. Just in time, six swans came swooping down. She threw the shirts upon them and her brothers became human again.

The girl and her brothers hugged each other, and she spoke. "Dear husband, search your mother's rooms — I am sure you will find our baby!"

Sure enough, they found him there safe and sound. The king's mother was asked to leave the kingdom, while everyone else lived together in peace and joy at last.

The Ant and the Dove

Once upon a time, a thirsty ant went to the stream for a drink. However, as the ant reached down to take a sip, it fell in. It was on the point of drowning when a dove plucked a leaf and let it fall into the stream. The ant used the last of its strength to scramble on to the leaf, then floated safely to the bank, exhausted but alive. Soon afterwards, a bird-catcher came along and saw the dove sitting in the tree.

Unnoticed by the dove, he set a trap for her. But the tiny ant saw what he had done. It raced up to the bird-catcher and bit him as hard as it could. The bird-catcher cried out, and the noise startled the dove, who flew off, safe and free.

Kindness brings rewards.

The Master of all Masters

Aservant girl went to a fair to find work, and luckily enough an old gentleman hired her. When they were back at his house he told her that he had his own, very particular names for many things and she would have to learn them. Then he asked her what she would call him.

"Why, master or mister, or whatever you please sir," she said.

"You must call me 'master of all masters'," he replied, before pointing to his bed. "And what would you call this?"

"A bed or whatever you please, sir."

"No, that's my 'barnacle'. And what do you call these?" he said pointing to his pantaloons.

"Breeches or trousers, or whatever you please, sir."

"You must call them 'squibs and crackers'. And what would you call her?" pointing to the cat.

"Cat or kit, or whatever you please, sir."

"You must call her 'white-faced simminy'. And this," showing the fire, "what would you call this?"

"Fire or flame, or whatever you please, sir."

"You must call it 'hot cockalorum'. What would you call this?" he went on, pointing to some water.

"Water or wet, or whatever you please, sir."

"No, 'pondalorum' is its name. And what do you call all this?" asked he, as he pointed to the house.

"House or cottage, or whatever you please, sir."

"You must call it 'high topper mountain'."

The girl thought him very strange but decided to stay. But that very night she woke up to find the house full of smoke! She woke her master up, shouting "Master of all masters, get out of your barnacle and put on your squibs and crackers. For white-faced simminy has got a spark of hot cockalorum on its tail, and unless you get some pondalorum, high topper mountain will be all on hot cockalorum!"

And they escaped unharmed!

The Tree and the Reed

There was once a **huge tree** that towered over its neighbours. At its foot grew a reed, slender and delicate. The two often talked to each other, and one day the tree said, "Well, little one, why don't you ever grow taller?"

"I am very content with my lot," said the reed. "I may not be grand, but I think I am safer."

"Safe!" sneered the tree. "Look at me – no one would be able to pull me up, but they could easily do that to you!"

Soon after, the tree had reason to regret its words. A hurricane tore it down, leaving little more than a pile of branches. But the little reed was able to bend before the force of the wind. And as soon as the storm was over, it stood straight up again.

Obscurity often brings safety.

How to Choose a Bride

A **man wanted to marry** but he didn't know how to choose a bride. He knew of three sisters, all of whom he liked, but he didn't know who would suit him best. He asked his mother's advice, and she said, "See how they eat cheese, then decide." So he invited them all to a meal with him.

When the cheese was served, the eldest cut the rind off so thick that it included a lot of good cheese. 'She seems wasteful,' thought the man.

The second sister ate her cheese without cutting off any of the rind at all. 'She is not right either,' thought the man. 'She will be careless.'

But the youngest sister cut the rind off cleanly and carefully, and then ate the cheese. The man knew at last, 'She is the right one!'

Hansel and Gretel

Long ago, a woodcutter lived in a forest with his two children, Hansel and Gretel.

The family were very poor — so poor that the time came when they didn't have enough to eat. The man's wife persuaded him to take the children into the wood and leave them there, so there were fewer mouths to feed. The woodcutter was shocked but he saw no other option. He did as his wife asked.

Hansel and Gretel were scared to be left alone in the dark forest. Cold and scared, they walked all night but they could not find their way out.

At last they glimpsed a little house. They couldn't believe their eyes — it was made of gingerbread! The starving children broke bits off and tucked in. Suddenly the door opened and an old witch came out.

She seized Hansel and locked him in a cage. Then for four weeks the witch forced Gretel to fetch water and cook meals for Hansel, for she wanted to fatten him up. Every morning the witch hobbled to the cage and cried, "Hansel, stick out your finger so I can see if you are fat enough to eat!" And every morning Hansel stuck out a little chicken bone, so she thought he was still thin.

One day the witch grew tired of waiting. "Time for a tasty meal of little boy," she announced. "Girl – go and climb inside the oven, to see if it is hot enough." The wicked old woman meant to shut Gretel in and cook her first, but Gretel was clever, "Can you show me how?" she said.

The witch grumbled but stuck her head in the oven. Then Gretel gave her a push and – clang! – she shut and bolted the door. The brave girl raced to the cage and set Hansel free. Then they filled their pockets with the witch's treasure and made their way home. There they found their father alone in the house – their wicked mother had died. He was overjoyed to see them, and they lived happily ever after.

The King's New Turban

Once, a man came before a great king and said, "Your Highness, I shall weave you a turban so special that only those who are truly intelligent shall be able to see it."

The king was intrigued by the idea, and said he would like to see such a thing.

After a long while, the man returned. "Here is your priceless turban, great King."

The king tore off the paper and saw... nothing. He didn't want to admit that he wasn't intelligent, so he forced a smile and handed over a great deal of gold to the man. All the nobles who were standing there agreed saying, "How beautiful!"

Then the king summoned his two closest advisors and whispered, "I must be a great fool, for I cannot see the turban!"

They admitted, "O King, nor can we!"

Then they rushed to catch the weaver and have him thrown into prison. But the weaver was gone!

Why the Bear is Stumpy-tailed

Bruin the Bear met Reynard the Fox on a roadside. He was slinking along with a string of fish that he had stolen from a farmer.

"Where did you find those?" asked Bruin.

"Oh, I've been out all day fishing and caught them," lied Reynard.

Bruin decided he would learn to fish too. "Oh, it will be easy for you," answered Reynard. "Just go out on the ice, cut a hole and stick your tail down into it. Then hold it there as long as you can. When you can wait no longer, pull your tail out!"

Bruin did as Reynard said, and held his tail a long time down in the hole, till it was frozen in. Then he pulled it out — and it snapped off!

And ever since then every bear has had a stumpy tail.

Foolish Hans

Once upon a time there was a poor woman and her foolish son, who was named Hans.

The woman gave Hans a big pot of honey to sell at the market, saying, "Sell this, but don't let people talk to you too much." She was afraid that people would bargain with him and he would be outwitted.

Arriving in town, he shouted, "Buy my honey!"

The people said, "How much is it?"

Foolish Hans said, "You are talking to me too much!" and he left town to head home.

Out in the country the flies swarmed around him.

"Buy my honey!" he said. The flies buzzed and he poured his honey on the ground saying, "Now pay me!" But they gave him nothing.

"Right!" he said. "I am reporting you to the judge. The flies have robbed me!"

He went to the court and said, "The flies bought my honey and they won't pay me."

The judge began to laugh, and said. "All I can say is that whenever you see a fly you should kill it."

But just then a fly flew onto the judge's nose, and Hans hit it really hard.

"Ouch! My nose!" cried the judge.

Hans said simply, "I was hitting at the fly, not at your nose."

Then the judge thought, 'He could kill someone if he sees a fly sitting on them.' So he paid Hans for the honey himself and Hans went home happily.

The Cat and the Birds

There once lived a cat who heard that the birds living in a nearby aviary had fallen ill. The cat decided that this would be the ideal opportunity for him to catch them, so he disguised himself as a doctor and set off for the aviary.

Once there, the cat presented himself at the door, and enquired after the health of the birds.

"We shall be much better," they replied, without letting him in, "when we have seen the last of you."

A villain may disguise himself, but he will not deceive the wise.

The Norka

Many years ago, a king and queen lived happily with their three sons until one day a Norka – a monster with mighty claws and sharp red teeth – came to the kingdom. The royal family knew that their people would not be safe until the Norka was dead.

After the two elder brothers had both tried to kill it and failed, it became the turn of the youngest son, Prince Ivan. He set out one evening to find it, and headed to the forest where it had last been seen.

At midnight the earth began to shake, and the Norka came rushing through the trees. Prince Ivan charged at the beast but it escaped down a long, long hole. He followed it, and at the bottom of the hole was another world, deep underneath the earth. Prince Ivan

walked until he saw a palace made of
gold, then knocked loudly at the
door. The lady who answered
was more beautiful than can
be imagined and the prince
fell in love with her at first
sight. When she saw him she
was delighted, and said, "Oh
Prince – why have you come
here?"

He told her about the
Norka, and she said she
was a princess from a
faraway land, "It
captured me many
years ago. No one has
been able to defeat the
cruel beast, even though many
have tried. It is currently asleep on a rock out in the
blue sea. Please conquer it!"

She then gave Prince Ivan a sword of steel and
told him that the only way to truly defeat the Norka
was to cut off its head with a single stroke.

The prince was as determined as ever to defeat
the monster, so he journeyed on, and saw the Norka

on a stone in the middle of the sea, as the princess
had described. He went up to it bravely and before
the Norka even realized he was there, chopped off
its head!

After his victory, Prince Ivan returned to the
palace and asked the princess to marry him, and she
said yes! Then they travelled back to the upper
world, where they lived happily ever after.

The Cat Maiden

Venus, the goddess of beauty, was debating with the great god Zeus about whether it was possible for a living thing to change its natural habits and instincts. Zeus said yes, it was; however, Venus said it was impossible.

To test the question, Zeus turned a cat into a maiden, and arranged for her to get married. When the young couple sat down to the wedding feast, Zeus said, "See how perfectly she behaves. Who could tell that yesterday she was a cat? Surely her nature is changed?"

"Wait," replied Venus, and she conjured up a mouse. Immediately the bride tried to pounce upon it. "Ah, you see," said Venus. "You will have to agree that I am right after all!"

The true nature of a living thing will always show itself in the end.

Paddy Corcoran's Wife

Paddy Corcoran's wife had been poorly for many years. She lay bedridden, trying medicines of all sorts, until Paddy was nearly brought to despair.

Then one day, a tiny woman dressed in a neat red cloak came in, and said, "Kitty Corcoran, you've had a long lie of it there on the broad of your back for seven years, and you're as far from being cured as ever."

"Yes" said the Kitty, "that's what I was just thinking about."

"It's your own fault," said the little woman. "All the time you've been ill, your children have thrown your dirty water out after dusk and before sunrise, at the very time we're passing your door, which we do twice a day. Now, if you avoid this and throw it out in a different place, at a different time, the sickness will leave you." The tiny woman then disappeared. Kitty did as she was asked, and the next day she found herself in perfect health once more — to the delight of her husband.

My Own Self

A poor widow once lived with her son in a tiny house far from any town or village. One night, there was a great, raging storm. The widow knew that on such a night, fairies were bound to be up to mischief so she told her son to go bed. But he was a very naughty boy, and refused to do so. After a while she gave up, and went to bed herself. Soon after her door shut the boy heard a fluttering sound in the chimney, and down by his side dropped a tiny girl with wings.

"Oh!" said the boy, "What do they call you?"

"My own self," she said, "What do they call you?"

"Just my own self too!" And with that they began to play together – the fairy made moving animals, tiny houses and little people out of the ashes. As the boy watched, he stirred the coals to make them blaze, and out jumped a hot cinder, which fell on the fairy's tiny foot.

She squealed so loudly that the boy clapped his hands to his ears. Then he bolted to his bed and hid under the blankets, listening in fear.

Then a sharp voice came from the chimney, "Who's there, and what's wrong?" it said.

"It's my own self," sobbed the fairy, "and my foot's burnt. Oh how it hurts!"

"Who did it?" said the voice angrily, and the boy, peeping from under the covers, could see a tiny white face looking out from the chimney-opening.

"Just my own self too!" said the fairy.

"If you did it your own self," cried the fairy-mother, "why make all this fuss about it?"

With that she reached out and caught her daughter by the ear, and pulled her up the chimney.

The next evening, the boy's mother was ever so surprised to find that he was happy to go to bed when she asked!

Give Me Nothing!

A woodman was carrying a heavy sack full of wood on his back when he tripped over a stone and half fell out. A passer-by asked, "What will you give me if I replace those pieces of wood?"

"Nothing," said the woodman.

"That's acceptable," agreed the other man. He replaced the wood then asked for his payment. The woodman was baffled.

"I told you I'd give you nothing," he said.

"Yes. And that's what I want. Give me nothing!"

After some quarrel, the two men went to the judge. He listened to both men and considered, gravely. He said to the passer-by, "Go and look under the carpet. What do you see there?"

"Nothing." said the man.

"Well, take it and go home," commanded the judge, "That is your payment!"

King Midas has Asses' Ears

In the time of ancient Greece, King Midas made the mistake of offending Apollo, the sun god, so the god gave him asses' ears instead of his own as a punishment. King Midas hid his ears under a turban so no one saw them, except his hairdresser, who promised to keep it secret. One day, however, the hairdresser was dying to tell the secret, so he went to a field, dug a hole and whispered it to the earth.

Soon after, a bed of reeds grew up. A musician came and made a pipe out of one of the reeds. He went to King Midas' court and when he played his pipe it sang out, "King Midas has asses' ears". The secret was a secret no longer, so King Midas took off his turban at long last.

The Hound and the Hare

There was once a young hound who sniffed out a hare and chased her at full pelt until he had caught up with her. The hare was terrified, waiting for death and wondering why the hound did not finish her off. One moment he would lunge at her and snap with his teeth as though he were about to kill her — even grabbing her coat in his jaws. Then the next he would let her go and leap about playfully, as if having fun with another dog.

The tormented hare grew more desperate until at last she gasped, "I wish you would show your true colours. If you are my friend, why do you bite me? If you are my enemy, why do you play with me?"

Anyone who plays double is not a true friend.

A French Puck

Puck was a very naughty spirit, who liked to change his shape and play tricks on people for fun.

One day, he became a fly and listened to a conversation between a couple who were about to be married. "Oh no!" said the woman, "I have forgotten to buy thread for my wedding dress!" But just as she spoke these words a large ball of thread appeared by the side of the road. It was made up of every colour you could think of. The man picked it up and took it to the dressmaker, who was delighted with it. It matched the dress perfectly.

On the couple's wedding day a great crowd assembled to witness the ceremony. The doors were opened, and the bride could be seen from afar.

"What a lovely dress!" whispered everyone. But just as she entered the church... Crick! Crack! Crick! Crack! The wedding dress fell to the ground.

Cloaks were offered to the young bride, and they were still married, but she was so upset that she could hardly stop the tears. One of the guests stayed behind to examine the dress and found that the thread had vanished! Mischievous Puck!

FEBRUARY

The Vixen and the Lioness

A lioness and a vixen were talking about their young, as mothers often do.

"My children are the picture of health," said the vixen, proudly.

"Well, my child has a particularly splendid coat," said the lioness, "and his mane is clearly going to be quite a sight to see."

"Everyone tells me how my children are the image of their parents," said the vixen.

"And I am often told that my son is clearly going to be as strong as his father," insisted the lioness.

"It's an absolute joy to see my cubs playing together," said the vixen, then she added, "but I notice you never have more than one."

"That's true," said the lioness with a steely glint in her eye, "but that one grows up to be the King of the Beasts."

Quality, not quantity.

The Old Woman and her Pig

An old woman bought a little pig from the market, but on her way home she came to a stile, and the pig would not jump over it. The old woman saw a dog nearby and had an idea. "Dog! Bite pig," she said. "Pig won't jump over the stile."

The dog wouldn't bite, however, so she went a little further, and found a stick. She said, "Stick! Poke dog – dog won't bite pig and pig won't jump the stile!" But the stick wouldn't do as she asked either! She travelled on and met a fire, but the fire wouldn't burn the stick. Then she met some water, but the water wouldn't quench the fire. Next she met a horse, but the horse wouldn't drink the water.

She went a little further, and she met a rope – but the rope wouldn't lasso the horse. And the little rat she met next wouldn't gnaw the rope!

But then she came
across a cat and said,
"Cat! Cat! Scare rat. Rat
won't gnaw rope, rope
won't lasso horse, horse
won't drink water, water won't
put out fire, fire won't burn stick,
stick won't beat dog, dog won't
bite pig, and pig won't jump
over the stile."

"All right," said the cat,
thoughtfully, "if you get me some milk."

The old woman fetched a saucer of milk at once,
and after the cat had had a drink, it scared the rat,
then the rat gnawed the rope, the rope lassoed the
horse, the horse drank the water, the water put out
the fire, the fire burnt the stick, the stick beat the
dog, the dog bit the pig, the pig jumped over the stile
— and that is how the old woman got
home before midnight!

The Fox and the Mask

There was once a fox who got into the storeroom of a theatre. He examined the scenery, costumes and props, wondering what everything was.

The fox was delighted when he came across what looked like a leg of chicken and a hunk of cheese, but when he bit into them — yuk! He found they were only made of paper and glue. As he turned to see if he could find any real food, the fox saw a face glaring down at him. He sprang back in fear, but the face didn't move. The fox became a little bolder and stopped shrinking back — still the face did not do so much as blink. Then the fox stepped closer — the face did not flinch. He stuck his tongue out and blew a raspberry. It was only a mask, the type actors use to put over their faces. "Ah," said the fox, "you look very fine. It's a pity you don't have any brains."

A fair face is of little value without sense.

Nasreddin Hodja and the Tax Collector

One day, a tax collector fell into the river. He didn't know how to swim so the villagers gathered by the river bank trying to save him.

"Give me your hand, give me your hand," they were all shouting. But the man did not hold out his hand. At that time Nasreddin Hodja walked by.

"Help!" said the villagers, "the tax collector is going to drown. He won't give us his hand."

"Let me try," said Nasreddin. "Here, you," he yelled to the man, "Take my hand!" The tax collector immediately held out his hand and grabbed Nasreddin Hodja's arm. The people around then pulled him out of the water.

"You see," Nasreddin Hodja explained, "You said, 'Give me your hand.' I said, 'Take my hand.' He is a tax collector – he is much better at taking than giving."

The Young Giant

Many years ago, there lived a farmer and his wife. They had a son who was no bigger than a thumb, so they called him Tiny Tom.

But one day a giant came along. He scooped up Tiny Tom and took him home! The giant didn't do him harm, far from it in fact. Instead, he fed him up for six years until he too became a big strong giant.

After this Tiny Tom returned to his parents, who were amazed at the change in their son. His mother gave him a huge pot of food, but it just wasn't

enough for his enormous appetite. Tiny Tom soon realized his parents couldn't keep him, so he decided to go into the world to seek his fortune.

He said goodbye to his parents and travelled over hill and dale and eventually came to a small farm where the farmer was looking for a chief woodcutter. "How much do you want as pay?" the farmer asked. To his astonishment, the giant replied, "Nothing… only after I have worked for you for a year, you must let me hit you two times."

The farmer and his wife thought the strange bargain was some sort of joke and they were very pleased that they would not have to pay him. "Very well," they agreed.

Next day, Tiny Tom started work. Early in the morning, all the farmhands started getting ready to go into the woods to chop down trees but Tom stayed in bed until midday. Then he got up, and slowly ate a huge breakfast. Only then did he stomp off into the forest after the other workers had been hard at work. He met them as they were on their way home for the day, leading horses that pulled carts full of the logs they had cut. But the young giant wasn't worried. He just ripped trees out of the earth, tossed them like matchsticks into a cart and

pulled it back to the
farm much faster than any
horse could, overtaking the other
workers on the way. The farmer was
delighted.

Tiny Tom served the farmer for a
whole year — and then, when the other workers were
getting their wages, it was time for him to have his
two hits.

"Stand still," he said to the farmer, and the young
giant hit him with such force that the farmer flew up
into the air and didn't come down. Then the young
giant hit the farmer's wife up into the sky too.

Whether they are still up there, hovering about, I
do not know. But what I can tell you is that Tiny
Tom took over at the farm and became the most
successful, happiest man for miles around.

The Greedy Brownie

There was once a brownie who loved playing tricks, as most brownies do. One day, he passed a dairy and thought it would be a good place to rest.

But his sleep was soon disturbed by two girls, called Jean and Meg, who had come to steal a taste of the cream with a ladle. This gave the naughty brownie an idea!

He crept up behind the girls and blew out their candle so they had to drink in the dark. Then, as Jean lifted the ladle the brownie lapped up all the cream before it reached her mouth. Meg snatched the ladle and tried to have her turn, but the brownie once again got there first. Jean snatched back the ladle from Meg. On it went, until the brownie was full of cream — the girls didn't get a drop!

Just then the farmer's wife entered. She believed the girls were the culprits and scolded them for their naughtiness, while the little brownie ran away laughing.

Cinderella

Long ago, there was a rich man whose wife had sadly died, leaving him with a young daughter. He soon married again, but his new wife was a bad-tempered woman. She had two daughters a little older than his own, who turned out to be just as nasty as their mother. When the man's daughter was older she was made to work very hard in the kitchen. Her stepmother made her sleep in the ashes of the fireplace and, because she was always dirty with cinders, they called her Cinderella.

One day, news arrived from the king that there was going to be a ball for the prince. All the young ladies in the country were invited, so that the prince could choose a bride. The two stepsisters were delighted and immediately started to order

Cinderella about: "Brush my hair! Iron my dress!"
When they were ready, they flounced off with their
stepmother to the palace. The minute they left the
house, Cinderella began to sob, but just then a
friendly-looking old woman appeared, and said,
"Don't cry, Cinderella. I'm your fairy godmother and
you shall go to the ball."

The fairy godmother turned a pumpkin
from the vegetable patch into a carriage,
and with a flick of her wand she changed
Cinderella's rags into a beautiful golden
dress. She soon set off for the palace,
and when she arrived the prince was
enchanted. He took her by the
hand and danced with her
all night. She looked so
different that no one
recognized her, not even
her stepsisters and
stepmother!

Cinderella knew
she had to leave
before midnight,
as her fairy
godmother had

warned her that the spell would end as the clock chimed twelve. So when it became late she slipped away – but one of her shoes fell off as she ran. The prince chased after her but she was too quick!

He was determined, however, to find the beautiful stranger he had fallen in love with, so the very next day he set out to find the girl the shoe fitted.

He went from house to house, but no girl could squeeze her foot into the dainty shoe. The prince was losing hope when he arrived, at last, at Cinderella's house. How disappointed he was when he saw the two ugly stepsisters! "Do you have any other daughters?" he asked Cinderella's stepmother.

At just that moment Cinderella came into the room. She sat down and put her foot into the shoe – and it fitted perfectly.

"This is my bride!" The prince cried. At once a grand wedding was arranged, and they lived happily ever after!

The Days of the Week

The days of the week decided to have a fancy-dress party, just for fun.

Sunday came dressed up as a priest about to go to church. Monday was a schoolboy because school starts on Monday. Tuesday was a warrior holding a sword in his hand. "Tuesday comes from the name of the Viking god of combat, Tyr," he explained. Wednesday turned up as a prince, with a golden crown on his head. Thursday also dressed as a warrior. "I am named after the Viking god of thunder, Thor," he said. Friday came dressed in a long robe. "My name comes from the Viking goddess of love, Freya," she smiled. Saturday dressed as a housewife and brought a big plate of sandwiches with her. Then the party got under way — and a very good time they had too!

The Two Soldiers and the Robber

There were two soldiers travelling together on a road one day when they were set upon by a robber. One of the soldiers ran away, however the other drew his sword and put up such a fight that the robber himself bolted.

When the coast was clear, the first soldier returned, yelling, "Where is he? Let me at him."

The brave soldier replied, "You are a little late, my friend. I only wish you had backed me up just now. Calm yourself, and put away your weapon. You may delude others into thinking you're as brave as a lion, but I know that at the first sign of danger, you run away like a hare."

It is no good pretending to be brave after the event.

Pandora's Box

Long ago in Greece, Zeus made the first woman to keep the first man company. The gods gave her many gifts including wisdom, kindness and beauty. Her name, Pandora, means 'All-gifts'. Zeus gave her a sealed box, and he warned her never to open it.

For a long time Pandora and her husband lived in great happiness. But the thought of the sealed box kept nagging at her mind. One day, she decided to open it, just a crack.

The second she lifted the lid, a host of terrible swarming, biting creatures rushed out. They were all the evils that cause suffering – war, illness, cruelty, spite and the rest. Luckily, at the bottom of the box one creature remained. It was hope – the one thing that keeps people going when times are bad. So Pandora also let hope out into the world.

The Bremen Town Musicians

A donkey, a cat, a dog and a cockerel left their homes and decided to go to Bremen to become musicians. It was too far to walk in one day to reach the town that evening, so as night fell they looked for a place to sleep. Soon they came to a little house. The donkey went to the window and looked in.

"My goodness," he gasped. "There's all sorts of good things to eat and drink – but there is a gang of robbers inside!" The animals stood on each other's shoulders to get a look, but they overbalanced and crashed through the window, making a terrible racket. The frightened robbers took flight, and as soon as they were gone the animals made themselves comfortable and went to sleep.

But the youngest robber crept back to see what had caused the noise. Nervously, he tiptoed up to the house and gently pushed open the door. He went to light a match from the coals and at once the cat flew in his face, spitting and scratching. The robber ran to the back door, but the dog sprang up and bit him on the leg. He leapt outside, where the donkey gave him a kick with its hind foot. Then the cockerel, which had been awakened by the noise, cried down from a beam in the roof, "Cockadoodledooooo!"

The youngest robber ran back to his captain as fast as he could, and said, "There is a horrible witch sitting in the house, who scratched my face with her long claws. By the back door stood a man with a knife who stabbed me in the leg. In the yard lies a monster who beat me with a wooden club. And above, on the roof, sat a ghost who screeched and wailed!"

After this the robbers never dared go back to the house again. But it suited the animals so well that they lived there happily for the rest of their days.

The Mischievous Dog

A man once had a dog that was a faithful companion to him. However, whenever visitors came to the man's house, the dog would bark and snap at them. The man of course found this a great nuisance so he fastened a bell around the dog's neck. This way, as people approached his house, they would hear the dog coming and be warned to stay back. The dog was very proud of the bell. He strutted about tinkling it with great satisfaction, showing it off as if it were a medal.

One day an old dog came up to him and said, "The fewer airs you give yourself the better. You don't think, do you, that your bell was given as a reward? No, it is a badge of disgrace."

Notoriety is often mistaken for fame.

In Times of Danger

Three fish, whose names were Plan Ahead, Think Fast, and Wait and See lived together in a pond. One day they heard a fisherman plan to fish in their pond the very next day.

Plan Ahead said, "I'm swimming away tonight!"

Think Fast said, "I'm sure I'll come up with a plan so I don't get caught."

Wait and See lazily said, "I just can't think about it now!"

When the fisherman cast his nets, Plan Ahead was long gone. But Think Fast and Wait and See were both caught! Think Fast quickly rolled onto his back and pretended to be dead. "Oh, this fish is no good!" said the fisherman, and threw him back. But Wait and See ended up in the fish market. That is why they say,

In times of danger, plan ahead
or plan to think fast!

The Two Jewels

A mighty king of India once said to his admiring servants, "Whoever can go round my kingdom in the shortest possible time shall have one of these two jewels." One of the servants stood up, walked round the king, and said, "Sir, may I have the prize?"

"Why?" said the king.

"Why, you are the kingdom, are you not?" said the courtier.

The king was so pleased with his answer that he gave him both the jewels.

The Donkey and its Shadow

Many years ago a man was going on a long journey, so he hired a donkey to carry his luggage. The donkey's owner said he would load the animal, and be the driver.

All went well to begin with. They set off down the road, making good progress until the sun blazed overhead and they were forced to stop and rest.

The traveller wanted to lie down in the donkey's shadow, but the owner wouldn't let him – he said he had hired the donkey, not its shadow. The quarrel grew heated, until they came to blows. But, while the men were fighting, the donkey shed its cargo, took to its heels and was soon out of sight!

If you quarrel about something that is unimportant, you may well lose what is important.

The Three Wishes

A poor fisherman lived by the edge of the sea in a tumbledown old cottage with his wife, who was always grumbling.

One evening he caught a tiny fish. "Please throw me back into the sea," said the fish, "and I will grant you the first three wishes made in your cottage."

The fisherman ran all the way home and in great excitement told his wife about the tiny fish.

"Whoever heard of a talking fish? You must be daft," and she slammed down a plate of dry bread.

"I wish this was a plate of fine sausages, for I am so hungry," said the fisherman wistfully.

No sooner were the words out of his mouth than there in front of him was a plate of sizzling sausages! But instead of being pleased, his wife yelled, "Why couldn't you have wished for something better?

We could have had chests of gold! You old fool! I wish the sausages were at the end of your nose!"

Immediately the sausages were stuck on his nose. The fisherman and his wife pulled and pulled at the sausages, but it was no good. They were stuck fast. There was nothing for it, they would have to use the last wish.

"I wish the sausages would disappear," said the fisherman sadly, and they did in a flash. So there they sat, the poor fisherman and his grumbling wife. No delicious supper of sizzling sausages and, much worse, no magic wishes. The fisherman never caught the tiny fish again, and as far as I know, his wife never stopped grumbling.

The Delicious Soup

Once upon a time there was a poor little girl who often went hungry at home. Then one day she met an old woman, who gave her a magic pot. If you said, "Boil, little pot!" it cooked delicious soup, and it only stopped when you said, "Stop, little pot!" The little girl took the pot home, so her family could have good soup whenever they liked.

One day the little girl went out, and her mother said, "Boil, little pot!" She ate all she wanted, but when she wanted it to stop, she'd forgotten what to say. The soup filled the kitchen, then the house, and soon the whole street. Finally, the child returned and said at once: "Stop, little pot!"

Immediately it stopped — but whoever wishes to enter the village now must swim through the soup!

The Peacock and Hera

A long, long time ago, in the early days of the world, the gods and goddesses of Mount Olympus ruled over earth, sky and sea.

At this time there was a peacock who prayed earnestly to the goddess Hera, Queen of Mount Olympus. The peacock was more than happy with his beautiful looks, which all the other birds envied, but he longed to have a better singing voice to go with it. He had quite an ugly cry, and what he really wanted was the voice of a nightingale.

However, the great Hera refused. The peacock would not take no for an answer and continued to beg. "Please grant me this," he pleaded, "after all, I am your favourite bird."

But Hera just replied, "Be content with what you have."

One cannot be first in everything.

Mother Holle

There was once a woman who was cruel to her stepdaughter and made her do all the cooking and cleaning, while her own daughter did nothing.

The stepdaughter was going about her work one day when she dropped a spindle into the well. Fearing her stepmother's anger, she jumped in to rescue it. But instead of landing in the water she found herself in a meadow.

She set off and after a time she came to a house where an old woman sat outside. The woman said, "I'm Mother Holle. Stay with me and you will be rewarded. You must shake out my pillows every day, for that makes it snow on earth."

The old woman seemed very kind, so the girl

agreed to stay with her. She worked hard for a few months and the woman was pleased, but the girl missed her home. Mother Holle understood. She led the girl to a large door, and as she walked out, a shower of gold pieces fell on her. They stuck to her all over, so she was completely covered with gold!

"That is your reward for working so hard," Mother Holle explained, and she showed the girl her way home. The girl's stepmother was amazed to see her covered in gold when she arrived, and said to her daughter, "You go and get some gold too!" And she pushed her down the well.

When the lazy girl came to Mother Holle's house, she agreed to work for her straight away. The first day, she toiled hard, thinking of the gold, but by the second day, she started to be her usual lazy self. Mother Holle got cross and told her to go home. The girl was very pleased, for she thought it was time to be covered with gold. But as she stood beneath the doorway, a shower of thick, gooey, black tar poured all over her. "That's your reward," said Mother Holle, as she shut the door.

The Master and his Pupil

A clever man had a big black book, which he had forbidden his pupil ever to touch. One day, when his master was out, the lad sneaked into his study to look at the book. He opened it and read one line out loud.

A loud clap of thunder rolled through the room and there stood the demon Beelzebub.

"Set me a task!" he roared.

"Water the flower!" cried the lad in panic, pointing to a geranium. The monster brought water and poured it onto the flower – but he did not stop. Soon the floor was covered with water. "Enough, enough!" gasped the lad. But the monster took no notice. The water rose to the lad's knees, to his waist, to his chin. Suddenly, the master rushed in and spoke the words to end the spell. And he never left his book unlocked again.

The Wise Mamad who Always Told the Truth

Once upon a time there lived a wise man called Mamad who never lied. The king heard about him and decided to play a trick.

The king held his horse by the reins, placed his left foot on the stirrup and told Mamad to tell the queen he was going hunting. Mamad bowed and left. Then the king laughed, and said, "We won't go hunting and so Mamad will have lied."

But wise Mamad went to the queen and said, "The king said he was going hunting but I don't know if he finished mounting his horse after I left."

Then the next day the king told the queen, "The wise Mamad lied to you yesterday."

But the queen told him what Mamad had said, and the king realized that the wise man only tells what he has actually seen.

The Lion and the Boar

A lion and a boar came to a spring one morning. They argued over who should be the first to drink.

"I was here first," growled the boar.

"Not so," insisted the lion, "I arrived before you."

The quarrel continued, until the lion and the boar suddenly charged at one another. They fought furiously until, pausing to take a breath, they saw some vultures seated nearby. The beady-eyed birds were obviously waiting for one of them to be killed so they could feed upon the dead carcass.

"If you're thinking what I'm thinking," said the lion, "we'd better make up."

"Yes," agreed the boar, "I'd rather forget our quarrel and live, than be food for vultures."

Those who argue may be watched by others, who will take advantage of the loser.

Why the Manx Cat has no Tail

Noah had nearly finished leading all the animals into the ark when a cat decided that she would like to go mousing one last time.

Noah's wife called and called her, but she would not come. Cats are always contrary!

Noah began to shut the door, but just then up pranced the cat. She managed to slip through the gap but her tail was caught in the door as it slammed shut. The cat was very cross as her tail was cut off, but Noah told her it was her own fault.

Forty days later, the flood was over and Noah opened the door of the ark once more. First out was the cat, and she ran and ran until she found the Isle of Man, and there she stopped. Ever since then the cats from the Isle of Man have had no tails.

The Fish and the Hare

An old **man and his wife** lived together in a little village, next to a forest. One day, the man found a pot of gold and silver between the trees.

'Oh, what luck!' he thought. 'But I can't take it home because my wife will tell the whole world!'

So he made a plan. He went and bought a live pike and a live hare at the market. Then he returned to the forest and hung the pike up at the top of a tree and tied up the hare at the edge of a stream. Then he trotted merrily home.

"Wife!" he cried. "I've found a pot full of treasure in the forest! Come with me and we'll fetch it."

They set off at
once, and it wasn't
long before the couple came
across the pike flapping at the top of
the tree and the hare wriggling in the
water — and the wife was flabbergasted. They dug
up the pot and drove home again.

So now the old couple had plenty of money. But
the wife was very foolish, and told everyone about it.
The governor of the town heard the story and
decided to take the couple's riches for himself, so he
sent his secretary to tell the man to give it to him.

But the old man just shrugged his shoulders and
said, "What treasure? I know nothing about
treasure. Pardon me, but my wife is not in her right
mind, sir. Ask her how it happened."

"Well, Mr Secretary," cried the wife, "we were
driving through the forest, and we saw a pike at
home in the top of a tree and a hare living in the
stream—"

"What rubbish! Are you making fun of me?"
shouted the secretary, losing his temper. And he
turned on his heel and drove back to the town. So
the clever old man got to keep his money to himself.

The Cat Mill

Once upon a time, a troll lived on a hill above a mill. Every evening he would enter the mill and demand a large glass of beer, which he would drink noisily, while shouting loudly and throwing the flour sacks around.

One night a travelling bear trainer took shelter for the night in the mill with his bears. The troll arrived as usual and jumped onto the bears, thinking they would be easy to attack. However, they scratched him so badly that he was barely able to escape!

The troll never entered the mill again but one day, looking down from the hilltop, he saw the miller and shouted, "Miller, do you still have those mean cats?"

And that is how the mill came to be known as the Cat Mill.

The Dog and the Wolf

It was a hot day on the farm, and the sleepy dog was on guard at the gate. He tried to stay awake but it was no good. Just as his eyes shut a wolf pounced and suddenly, the dog was fighting for his life.

He begged for mercy, saying, "Wolf, I will make a wretched meal. But if you wait a few days, my master is giving a feast. The leftovers will be mine and I shall get nice and fat. That will be a better time to eat me." So the wolf let him go and sloped away.

As the dog had said, the feast took place and he ate his fill of tasty leftovers. The next day, the wolf arrived, only to find the dog out of reach on the stable roof.

"My friend," the dog said, "if you catch me down there again, don't wait for any feast."

Once bitten, twice shy.

Brabo and the Giant

Years ago, a rough and cruel giant named Antigonus lived on the banks of the river that flowed through Antwerp in Belgium.

Every day, hundreds of white-sailed ships sailed on the river, trading goods and making the city wealthy. But one day, the wicked giant built a strong castle on the riverbank with dark, damp dungeons.

The giant, with a big knotted club made out of an oak tree, strode through the town. "From this day," he roared, "no ship shall pass by this place without paying me. Whoever refuses, shall have both his hands cut off."

The people were terrified, and for a time they did as the giant said. The giant grew very rich while the city became poor. After a few months a brave young fellow named Brabo studied the castle and saw a window where he could climb up into the giant's chamber. Brabo went to the duke and promised that he would seek out and fight the ruffian if his lord's soldiers would storm the gates of the giant's castle and distract him.

The duke agreed and at the given signal, hundreds of men holding ship's masts, or tree trunks, marched against the gates. They smashed the iron-bound timbers and rushed in. Brabo climbed into the castle through a slit in the thick wall and sword in hand, snuck up on the monster, who had rushed to fight the men at the gates. Brave Brabo made a sweep with his sword and dealt a single deathly blow, and at last the giant was defeated.

That night every window of every house in Antwerp showed lighted candles to celebrate, and the city was bathed in light. After this, thousands of ships sailed peacefully and Antwerp became very rich again.

The Important Thing

A scholar, who studied many books, asked a boatman to row him across a river. As they started, the scholar said, "Tell me, boatman, what use you've made of your life. Have you ever studied history or science?'"

"No," said the boatman.

"Have you learnt languages? Or mathematics?"

"No," said the boatman, "not at all."

"Too bad," said the scholar, "Learning is the most important thing. You've wasted half your life."

Suddenly the rickety boat crashed into a rock in the middle of the river. The boatman turned to the scholar and said, "Wise man, tell me, have you ever learned to swim?"

"No," said the scholar, "I've spent my life thinking."

"Too bad," said the boatman, "You've wasted your life. For now the boat is sinking."

MARCH

The Eagle and the Beetle

An eagle was once chasing a hare, who was running for her life. As the hare sprinted, she saw a beetle and gasped for help. Although the beetle was tiny, he agreed. Sadly the eagle still caught the hare, but from then on whenever the eagle laid an egg, the beetle rolled it out of the nest.

After a few years of this the eagle went to the god Jupiter for help. Jupiter allowed the eagle to lay her eggs in his lap, where they would be safe. But the beetle had a plan. He made a ball of dirt the size of an eagle's egg, and placed it on top of the eggs in the god's lap. When Jupiter saw the dirt, he stood up to shake it out of his robe, and shook out the eggs too! Ever since then, eagles never lay their eggs in the season when beetles are about.

The weak can always find ways to avenge an insult, even upon the strong.

The Accomplished and Lucky Teakettle

A long time ago in Japan there was an old teakettle in a temple. One day, when the temple priest was about to hang it over the hearth to boil some water, the kettle suddenly sprouted the head and tail of a badger. What a wonderful kettle! It danced all over the room, and was impossible to catch.

But soon the priest found the kettle too much trouble and sold it to a tinker. The tinker was astounded to find that the accomplished teakettle could dance and walk a tightrope.

The tinker displayed the kettle in an exhibition that travelled the country. Everyone came to see it, even princesses and the emperor! The tinker soon grew so rich that he gave the kettle back to the temple, where it was put on show as a precious treasure and worshipped as a saint.

The Dog, the Cat and the Mice

In the beginning the cat and dog were friendly with each other, each doing their own work.

But then they drew up an agreement. They decided the dog would do the outside work, and the cat would do the work inside. Once it was settled upon, the cat put the agreement in the loft.

Everything was going well until one day the dog said he didn't see why he had to protect the house and get cold, whilst the cat was comfortable inside.

The cat said, "We had an agreement."

The dog replied, "Let me see it."

So the cat went up to the loft, but mice had eaten the agreement and it was just a heap of fluff.

The cat was furious. She chased the mice, killing as many as she could.

When the cat told the dog that she didn't have the agreement, the dog growled at her.

Since that time, whenever a dog meets a cat he asks her for the agreement, and as she cannot show it to him he goes for her. And the cat, knowing the mice ate the agreement, runs after them whenever she sees them.

The Horse, Hunter and Stag

A horse and a stag were great friends, but one day, they quarrelled badly and the friendship ended. The horse decided to seek revenge, so he asked a hunter for help. The hunter listened as the horse explained how he wanted him to kill the stag. "I will help you," the hunter said, "but to be successful, you must let me ride you."

The horse agreed, and the hunter soon saddled and bridled him. With the horse's speed, the hunter chased down the stag and killed it. The delighted horse thanked him. Then he said, "Now remove those things from my mouth and back."

"Not so fast," said the hunter. "Now I've got you I will keep you."

If you allow people to use you to get what you want, they may also use you to get what they want.

Nasreddin Hodja is Caught in a Lie

One day Nasreddin Hodja's neighbour came to him and said, "Nasreddin, we need a donkey for a few hours. Can I borrow yours?"

Nasreddin did not want to lend his donkey, so he thought quickly. Then he said, "I would gladly help, dear neighbour, but he is not here at the moment."

Just then the donkey's loud and long bray was heard from the shed.

"Shame on you," said the neighbour, "I've caught you out in a lie – your donkey is braying in his shed."

"My dear fellow," Nasreddin Hodja said calmly, "are you going to believe my word or are you going to believe a donkey?"

The Old Man and the Fairies

Many years ago, when the Welsh mountains were full of fairies, an old man was walking to a market. On the way he sat down to rest in a lonely valley, and dropped off into a deep sleep.

While he slept, the fairies came and carried him off under the earth. He awoke after a while and found himself in a great palace of gold, filled with fairies dancing and singing.

At the end of the night the fairies carried the man back to the valley, and when he looked in his bag he found it filled with gold! The man just managed to pick it up, and stagger home with it. His wife came out to greet him, and said, "Where have you been?"

He explained what had happened and showed her the gold. They agreed to go and spend it the very next day, but in the morning they found the bag was in fact full of cockleshells!

Snow White and the Seven Dwarfs

Once upon a time there was a little princess called Snow White. Her stepmother, the queen, was beautiful but cruel. She had a magic mirror, which could answer questions. The queen asked it who the fairest lady in the land was, and the mirror would always tell her that she was. But as Snow White grew up she became more lovely than her stepmother, and the mirror told the queen this.

Outraged, the queen ordered one of her huntsmen to kill Snow White. The huntsman could not bring himself to carry out this wicked task, so he abandoned Snow White in the woods.

Snow White wandered in the woods for hours, scared, until she came to the house of seven dwarfs, who kindly took her in and let her live with them.

They were all happy for a time, but then the mirror told the queen that Snow White was still alive and living in the woods.

The queen simmered with fury! The next day, after the dwarfs had gone to work, she disguised herself as an old pedlar, and went to the cottage, calling out, "Good laces, fine laces."

Snow White bought one that was made of silk.

"Let me lace you up properly," said the old pedlar, and she laced her up so quickly and tightly that Snow White fell to the floor as though dead.

Soon after, the seven dwarfs returned and cut the lace so that Snow White could breathe again.

When the queen got home her mirror told her that Snow White had been rescued, so the next day she made a poisoned comb and once more went in disguise to the dwarfs' cottage.

She soon persuaded Snow White to let her fix her hair, and the minute the queen touched her with the poisoned comb, Snow White fell to the floor as though dead.

Luckily the seven dwarfs came home just as the queen left, and they removed the comb. Snow White came back to life again.

When the queen found out that Snow White had been saved for a second time, she burnt with rage and returned to the cottage, this time dressed as an apple-seller. She gave Snow White a poisoned apple, and as soon as she took a bite, it choked her. The dwarfs returned home to find their beloved Snow White dead. They made a glass coffin, and laid Snow White in it. They set it in a beautiful glade.

Soon after, a prince came riding past. He asked the dwarfs if he could try to wake the girl and they agreed. As the prince's servants lifted the coffin up they stumbled and Snow White received such a jolt that the poisoned apple flew out of her throat and she began to breathe again!

It was love at first sight for the prince and Snow White, and soon a wedding was organized. They all lived happily ever after – all apart from the evil queen, who disappeared in a puff of smoke, never to be seen again.

The Bat, the Birds and the Beasts

There was a time when the birds and the beasts always argued. After a while the two sides decided to wage war on each other.

When the armies were ready, the bat hesitated about which to join. The birds said, "Come with us."

But the bat said, "I am a beast."

The beasts said, "Join us."

But the bat said, "I am a bird."

Luckily, peace was settled and no battle took place. The bat heard the birds celebrating.

"Can I join in?" he asked, but the birds flew at him angrily.

The beasts were also having a party. The bat again asked to join in and again was driven away.

"I see," said the bat, "I did not say I was one thing or the other, so now I don't fit anywhere."

He that is neither one thing or the other has no friends.

The Mice that Ate some Iron Scales

Long ago there was a man who had only a pair of valuable iron scales in his possession. He left them with a merchant for safekeeping while he travelled. When he returned, the man asked for his scales, but the merchant said, "They have been eaten by mice."

The man knew this was a trick and he was angry. He went off, sneaking the merchant's little boy with him. The merchant followed him to his house and said, "Where is my son?"

The man said, "A hawk carried him off."

The merchant replied, "That's impossible."

The man said, "If mice can eat iron, a hawk can carry a boy."

When the merchant heard this, he knew he was found out. He gave the man back his scales, and the man gave the boy back to the merchant.

Why the Tail of the Fox has a White Tip

An old woman was looking for a shepherd to watch her sheep when she met a fox.

"I will watch your sheep for you," said the cunning fox. And he went to work.

At the end of each day, however, one of the sheep was missing. "Where is my sheep?" the woman would ask and the fox would answer, "The wolf ate it."

One day the woman thought, 'Mr Fox must feel guilty. I'll take him a drink of cream.' She went to the field, and caught the fox attacking a sheep! "You cunning fox!" she cried.

The woman had nothing to throw at him but the cream, so she threw that. It struck the tip of his tail, and from that day to this, the tip of the fox's tail has been as white as cream.

The Hare-brained Crocodiles

Long, long ago, in Japan, on the island of Oki, there lived a little white hare. The hare was bored with life on the tiny island and wanted very much to cross over to the mainland. One day as usual, the hare was standing on the beach, looking towards the mainland when he saw a great crocodile swimming nearby. 'This is lucky!' thought the hare. 'I will ask the crocodile to carry me across the sea!'

But the hare knew that crocodiles could be dangerous so he thought of a trick.

He said, "Oh, Mr Crocodile, I know very little about you. Won't you come out of the sea and play on the shore?"

The crocodile had been feeling quite lonely, so he agreed.

"Tell me, do you think there are more crocodiles than hares?" said the hare, after a while.

"Of course, there are," answered the crocodile haughtily. "Can you not see that for yourself?"

So the hare said, "Do you think there are so many crocodiles that it is possible for you to call up enough to form a line across the sea to the mainland?"

The crocodile snorted and answered, "Of course."

"Then do try," said the artful hare, "and I will count them!"

The crocodile went off and reappeared, bringing with him a large number of other crocodiles.

"Look, Mr Hare," announced the crocodile proudly, "There are enough crocodiles to stretch from here as far as India!" Then the whole company of crocodiles arranged themselves so as to form a bridge between the Island of Oki and the mainland.

The hare hopped off the island on to the bridge of crocodiles, saying, "Now I'll count you," as he jumped from one crocodile to the next. "One, two, three, four, five, six, seven…" And so the cunning hare hopped right across the crocodiles to the mainland!

The Farmyard Cockerel and the Weathercock

Once upon a time, there was a weathercock on top of a farmhouse. Although he was so rusty that he no longer turned with the wind, he was very proud of his high position. He looked down on the hens, chicks and a fine cockerel in the yard below.

"Cockadoodledoo!" the farmyard cockerel crowed. "My chicks will grow up big and strong, just like their father," and he flapped his wings and crowed again.

"That farmyard cockerel is stupid," the weathercock said. "What is he good for? He can't even lay an egg!"

But then there came a mighty gust of wind and the weathercock snapped right off. His rusty old fixings had broken. He tumbled to the ground and had to lie there while the real birds pecked and scratched around him.

You're no good to anyone if you're worn out!

Odds and Ends

There was a girl who was pretty but very lazy. If, when she was spinning, there was a little knot in the flax, she would pull out a big hunk, and throw it away. She had a hard-working servant, however, who gathered the thrown-away bits of flax, spun them fine, and made beautiful dresses from the waste.

Now, the lazy girl was due to be married, and on the night before the wedding, there was a great party. The servant girl looked very beautiful, dancing in one of her dresses. As they watched, the bride said to her husband-to-be, "Look at her, all dressed in my odds and ends."

When the man asked the girl what she meant she explained that her servant was wearing a dress made of discarded flax. When the bridegroom heard how lazy she was, he gave her up and went to the servant, and asked her to be his wife instead.

Chicken Licken

One fine day an acorn fell on Chicken Licken's head and he panicked, thinking that the sky was falling in. He set off to tell the king, and on the way he met Henny Penny, Cocky Locky, Ducky Lucky and Drakey Lakey. They all said that they would come with Chicken Licken to see the king. Next they met Goosey Loosey and Turkey Lurkey — they said they would come as well, and on the way they met Foxy Loxy. "We are off to tell the king that the sky is falling in." Chicken Licken clucked importantly.

"I know the way," said Foxy Loxy with a cunning smile. "Follow me."

So they all set off behind Foxy Loxy. He led them all straight to his den where he ate them all up! So the king never heard that the sky was falling in (which it wasn't, of course).

The Poor Miller's Boy and the Cat

An old miller wished to retire, so one day he said to his three servants, "I will give the mill to whoever brings me the best horse."

So they all set off. Two of the men decided to team up and left the third, who was called Eric, alone. Trudging along a road on his own, he met a small grey cat. To his great surprise it spoke to him. "If you work as my servant for seven years, I will give you the most beautiful horse in the world."

So Eric went to the cat's enchanted castle, which was filled with her cat servants. They sat down to enjoy a meal together, and the grey cat told him his task would be to chop wood every day.

Eric stayed with the cats and worked hard, and was very content there. When the seven years were up, the grey cat said to him, "Go back to the mill, and in three days' time I will bring you a horse."

Eric set off down the road to the mill, where he met the other two servants. They had brought the miller old nags, and they mocked Eric for returning with nothing. But on the third day, a golden coach drove up pulled by six gleaming horses. Behind them, a groom rode upon a seventh. The miller thought this was the best horse he had ever seen, and said at once that Eric would inherit the mill.

Just then the coach came to a stop, and a beautiful princess stepped out. She told Eric, "I was the grey cat. By serving me faithfully for seven years you broke the enchantment upon me!"

So instead of becoming a miller, Eric married the beautiful princess, and the two lived happily ever after.

The Foolish Wise Man

A wise man, a bald man, and a barber were once travelling together. They stopped for the night and agreed to take turns keeping watch as it was a dangerous part of the country. It was the barber's turn first. He propped up the sleeping wise man, and, for a joke, shaved his head. When it was the wise man's turn to keep watch the barber woke him up. The wise man felt his bare head and shouted loudly at the barber, "What a fool you are! You have woken the bald man instead of me!" Perhaps he wasn't so wise after all!

The Fairy Fluffikins

The Fairy Fluffikins was the funniest little fairy you ever saw, but she was also very naughty. She tickled the baby dormice until they screamed with laughter, she filled the squirrel's nut stores with pebbles and teased the owl with a dead mouse on a string by pulling it away when he went for it. But one day she got into trouble herself.

She was poking about when she found a little house with wire walls and a wooden door. In she hopped, but it was a trap! There was a bang, the wooden door slammed, and Fluffikins was caught.

In the morning the farmer found her, and carried her home to his little girl. So if you call on Ann Smith you will see Fairy Fluffikins there in a little cage. And it serves her right!

The Wise Men of Gotham and the Cuckoo

The foolish wise men of Gotham loved to hear the call of the cuckoo in spring, so one year they decided to try and capture it. They thought that if they kept a bird in the village they could enjoy hearing its call all year round. The foolish men planted a thick hedge in a circle, and wove extra twigs into it to make it far too dense for a cuckoo to fly through. Finally they trapped a cuckoo, and put it inside the ring of hedges.

The men stood back proudly, pleased with their work. But of course, the first thing the cuckoo did was fly away up into the sky. The men of Gotham scratched their heads. "We didn't make the hedge high enough," they said sadly.

The Lion and the Bull

One day a lion passed by a field of cattle. Among them was a huge bull and the lion began to drool with hunger. He went away and thought hard about how he could get the bull into his clutches.

The next day the lion sent the bull an invitation to come to dinner. The bull was flattered at being asked, and he accepted at once.

That evening the excited bull made his way to the lion's den. The lion told the bull to make himself at home. But the bull looked carefully around him. He noticed at once that there was little sign of anything cooking, and left. The lion called out after him to ask his reason for going. The bull called back, "When I saw your kitchen it struck me at once that dinner was to be a bull."

If you lay your plans in front of your enemies, you will fail.

The Three Little Pigs

There were once three little pigs who decided to make their own way in the world. The first little pig set out and built a house of straw, but along came a big bad wolf.

"Little pig, little pig, let me come in!" shouted the big bad wolf.

"No, not by the hair on my chinny chin chin. I'll not let you in," squeaked the first little pig.

"Then I'll huff and I'll puff, and I'll blow your house down," yelled the wolf. And he did. He huffed and he puffed and he blew the straw house down. The first little pig squealed and ran away as fast as she could, before the wolf could catch her.

Meanwhile, the second little pig built a house out of sticks. Along came the big bad wolf. "Little pig, little pig, let me come in!" shouted the wolf.

"No, not by the hair on my chinny chin chin. I'll not let you in," squeaked the second little pig.

"Then I'll huff and I'll puff, and I'll blow your house down," yelled the wolf. And he did. The second little pig escaped just in time.

Now, the third little pig had built a house out of bricks, and he lived there very happily. Then along came the big bad wolf. "Little pig, little pig, let me come in!" shouted the wolf.

"No, not by the hair on my chinny chin chin. I'll not let you in," squeaked the third little pig.

"Then I'll huff and I'll puff, and I'll blow your house down," yelled the wolf. And he tried. He huffed and he puffed but he could not blow the brick house down. He climbed down the chimney, but fell into the big pot of boiling water that the clever little pig had placed on the fire — and that was the end of him!

The third little pig found his brother and sister, and they all lived happily together in the little brick house.

The Toad's Godmother

Two girls were walking along a path when a huge toad waddled in front of them. One of the girls joked that if the toad ever had a baby, she would be its godmother. The other one added that she would cook for the occasion.

A few days later the girls met an old woman who reminded them of their promise, and asked them to come to the baptism of the toad's child. She led them to the toad's house. The first girl was appointed godmother, and the other cooked a fine feast. Then the woman sent them on their way, and gave them a bag of coal.

As they walked, they let most of the coal fall to the ground as it was quite heavy. But when they got home, they saw that the little bit of coal they still had was pure gold — how they wish they had kept it all!

The Lion, the Fox and the Beasts

The lion once fell very ill, so he summoned all the animals to him so he could tell them his last wishes.

First, the goat came to the lion's cave.

He was gone a long time, so a sheep decided to go in when the sheep didn't return. A calf also decided to enter the cave to hear the lion's last wishes when the sheep didn't return.

After a while, the lion appeared outside. Strangely, he was feeling stronger. He saw a fox waiting. "Why did you not come to see me?" he snarled.

"I beg your pardon," said the fox, "but I noticed the tracks of the animals that had entered the cave. And while I see many going in, I can't see any coming out. Until all the animals come out, I will stay here."

It is easier to fall into an enemy's clutches than to get out again.

The Nightingale

The emperor of China lived in the most splendid palace in the world surrounded by a large, beautiful garden. In the forest nearby there lived a nightingale and all the world praised its song.

When the emperor was told of its beautiful singing he demanded it be brought to him. The nightingale sang sweetly, and the emperor was entranced. He built it a golden cage and listened to its song every day. But then, one day, the Emperor of Japan sent the king the gift of a golden clockwork bird, encrusted with jewels, that moved and sang when you wound it up. It only had one song that was always the same, but the emperor loved his new toy and didn't notice when the real nightingale flew away back to the forest.

Years passed. The emperor fell sick, and it seemed nothing could save him. As he lay on his deathbed, he begged to hear the golden notes of his toy bird one last time, but when they wound it up, it was found to be broken and couldn't sing.

As the emperor sank towards death, a bird flew in through the window and started to sing. It was the real nightingale, returned to help the man who had loved it once, and it sang so sweetly that all the king's sickness passed from him. When the courtiers came in the next morning, the king greeted them, alive and well.

The Donkey and the Old Peasant

An old peasant was on a journey with his donkey, which he was driving along with a stick. All his belongings were strapped to the poor animal's back.

The peasant decided to have a rest when all of a sudden he caught sight of armed men stealthily approaching.

The terrified peasant jumped onto the donkey's back, begging it to run as fast as it could. But the donkey did not budge. It said, "Do you think those men will make me carry heavier loads than I have now?"

"Probably not," said the peasant.

"Oh well," said the donkey, "I don't mind if they do take me, for I shan't be any worse off."

And it returned to nibbling the grass, leaving its master to his fate.

It's better to settle for the lesser of two evils.

The Kindness of the Fire God

There once lived a very rich man who set out on a long journey. On the way he met a woman, dressed in red, who begged him to take her with him. The rich man kindly agreed, helped her onto his wagon, and they set off together.

They had not gone far when the woman said, "I am the Fire God. As you are a good man I will give you this warning — tomorrow a fire will break out in your house. Hurry home and save what you can!" With that, she vanished.

The man drove home as fast as he could. Just as he removed the last of his possessions from his house, a fire broke out and raged until the whole building burnt down. The man thanked goodness for the Fire God's warning!

The Crow and the Pitcher

There was a crow who had been unable to find water for many days – not even a drop. Imagine his amazement and joy when he suddenly came upon a water pitcher.

However, when the crow put its beak into the mouth of the pitcher he found that he could not reach far enough down to get to the water. He tried and tried, but at last had to give up in despair.

Then a clever thought occurred to him, and he took a pebble and dropped it into the pitcher. The water level rose slightly. Then he took another pebble and dropped it in. Then another, and another…

At last, the crow saw the water rise up near him, and after casting in a few more pebbles he was able to quench his thirst and save his life.

Little by little does the trick.

Nasreddin Hodja and the Delicious Stew

Nasreddin Hodja brought two kilograms of meat home one day, and asked his wife to cook a nice stew for dinner, then went off to work. Nasreddin's wife cooked the stew but at lunch time a few of her relatives visited. She served them the stew, and they finished it all.

When Nasreddin came home and asked his wife if the stew was ready she said, "Ahh! Such trouble! The cat ate it."

Nasreddin Hodja looked around and saw the scrawny little cat, looking just as hungry as he felt himself. He grabbed the cat and weighed him. The poor thing weighed exactly two kilograms.

"Well," said the Hodja, "if this is the cat, where is the stew? And if this is the stew, then where is the cat?"

The Valiant
Little Tailor

A little tailor was sitting in his house one summer morning sewing when some flies came buzzing in. The tailor took off his shoe. *SLAM!* Seven flies were dead underneath — seven!

He was so proud he made himself a belt with the words: *7 AT ONE BLOW* stitched upon it. He locked up his little house and set off to spread the word of his deed around the world.

Another traveller noticed the tailor's belt. 'He must be a mighty warrior,' he thought and hurried to tell the king. The king was delighted and ordered the tailor to be brought before him at once, for he had an important task to give him.

"In the nearest forest there are two giants," the king told the tailor. "They cause all sorts of trouble. If you can get rid of them, I'll give you half of my kingdom and my daughter's hand in marriage!"

So the tailor set out and soon came to the forest. There were the two giants, sleeping under a tree, snoring. The little tailor climbed a tree and threw down a stone onto the chest of one. Immediately the giant woke up and gave his friend a shove. "Stop throwing things!" He roared.

"You must have gone mad," shouted the first giant, "I'm not throwing things at you!"

Next the tailor threw a really big stone at the other giant. He sprang up and punched his friend on the nose. The other hit him straight back – and so it went on, until at last they both fell down dead.

Then the little tailor hurried back. "It is done," he announced to the king. "Now where is my reward?"

The king had to keep his promise. And that is how a cheeky little tailor married a princess, won half a kingdom and became a king – all through swatting flies!

The Hungry Horse

A noble lord **wanted to give justice** to all his people, so he placed a bell with a piece of rope tied to it outside his gate. He promised that he would help anyone who rang the bell.

One day the bell rang loudly, and when the lord came out, he was surprised to find a starving old horse there, chewing the end of the rope. One of the bystanders told how the horse had belonged to a neighbouring knight. It had carried him safely through many battles, but now that it was old and useless its cruel master had turned it out.

The lord said the horse deserved a reward for its hard work, and ordered the knight to give it a place in his stable and plenty of food as long as it lived.

The Town Mouse and the Country Mouse

Once upon a time, a town mouse went to visit his
cousin in the country. The country mouse was
poor and lived a simple life. Cheese and bread, and a
bed of straw were all he had to offer.

The town mouse wasn't
impressed. "Come with me," he
said. "I'll show you how to live."

When they arrived at the town
mouse's house the town mouse
took his cousin into a splendid
dining room. There, they found
the remains of a fine feast on the table.

The mice were just tucking in when they heard a
loud growling. "What's that?" asked the country
mouse squeaking in terror.

"It is only the dogs of the house," answered the
town mouse.

"Only the dogs!" gasped the country mouse. "I'm
off home."

Better to live poorly in
peace than richly in fear.

Jorinda and Joringel

There was once an enchanted old castle that was home to a witch. If anyone came near it, they would be struck still like a statue, and if it was a girl that was trapped, the witch would change her into a rare bird. Her castle contained about seven thousand cages of the poor creatures!

One day, a betrothed couple – Jorinda and Joringel – went for a walk and strayed too near the witch's castle.

At once Jorinda disappeared and a nightingale appeared in her place, singing sadly. Joringel could do nothing for he was frozen as though made of stone.

A moment later, the witch came and caught the nightingale.

After she had left Joringel found himself able to move again, so he went to think what to do. That night Joringel dreamt that he found a blood-red flower. Nothing could harm him, for the flower broke every evil spell.

When Joringel woke, he went out searching for the flower. He looked high and low, and on the ninth morning he found it. He picked it and walked to the evil castle. Carrying the flower, he found he could enter unharmed, and he rushed to explore and find Jorinda.

At last he came to a vast room filled with cages. Just as he found his nightingale the witch leapt out at him, but when she was just three paces away she stopped — it was as if she had hit an invisible wall.

Joringel drew up his courage and took no notice of her. He touched the nightingale with the flower — and at once Jorinda was standing there, throwing her arms around him, as beautiful as ever. Then they used the flower to turn all the other caged birds back into maidens.

The pair were married the very next week. The blood-red flower brought them luck in everything they did, and they lived happily ever after.

APRIL

Nasreddin Hodja and the Parrot

One day Nasreddin Hodja was walking around the market place when he saw a brightly coloured bird. The price on it was twelve gold coins.

"How can a bird be so expensive?" Hodja asked the shoppers nearby in astonishment.

"It is a special bird," they explained, "for it can talk like a human!"

At this Hodja went straight home, grabbed his turkey and brought it to the market place. He stood near the man selling the parrot and yelled, "Turkey for sale! Only ten gold coins!"

"How can a turkey be worth ten gold coins?" the shoppers protested.

"There is a bird over there going for twelve," insisted Nasreddin.

"But that bird can talk like a human being," the people said. But Nasreddin didn't care. "And this turkey can think like a human being," he answered.

How the Rhinoceros got his Skin

Once upon a time, there lived a man who decided to bake a cake. When it was ready he took it down to the beach to eat, but suddenly a rhinoceros appeared!

Now, in those days the rhinoceros's skin fitted him quite tightly, with no wrinkles. In fact, he could take off his skin — it had three buttons underneath.

The rhino stomped right up to the man and said, "How!"

Of course the man was terribly frightened, so he dropped his cake and climbed straight to the top of a palm tree! The rhinoceros spiked the cake on his horn and ate it. Soon after, the man came down and said:

*"Them that takes cakes
Which the Man bakes
Makes dreadful mistakes."*

Five weeks later, there was a heatwave, and everybody took off their clothes. The rhinoceros took off his skin and left it on the beach. He waddled into the water to cool down.

Soon after the man came by. He took that skin, and he shook that skin, and he rubbed that skin full of dry, stale, tickly cake crumbs. Then he climbed up his palm tree and waited for the rhinoceros to come out of the water and put on his skin.

And the rhinoceros did. He buttoned it up, and it tickled like cake crumbs in bed! He ran to a palm tree and rubbed and rubbed himself against it. The rhino rubbed so much and so hard that his skin soon became wrinkled all over!

And he went home, very angry and horribly scratchy, and since then every rhinoceros has had great folds in his skin and a very bad temper.

The Two Pots

Two pots had been left on the bank of a river. One was made of brass and the other of earthenware. As the tide rose, they both floated off down the stream. They were tossed this way and that way by the current, and the earthenware pot tried its best to keep away from the brass one. Then the brass one cried out, "Don't worry my friend, I will not hit you."

"But I may bash into you by accident," said the earthenware pot. "Whether I hit you, or you hit me, you'll be fine, but I will suffer for it."

Equals make the best friends.

The Three Billy Goats Gruff

One day three billy goats Gruff decided to cross a bridge over a river, go up the hill and make themselves fat on grass. The smallest goat went first, but he was only halfway across when a troll appeared, roaring, "Who's that trit-trotting over my bridge? I'll gobble you up!"

The goat said, "Don't take me, I'm too little. Wait till my big brother comes," and ran across to safety.

When the second goat tried to cross, the troll once more roared out his threat. But the second goat just said, "Don't take me, I'm too bony. Wait till my big brother comes," and ran across to safety.

When the third Billy Goat Gruff stepped onto the bridge, the troll roared out again, "Who's that trit-trotting over my bridge?"

"ME!" said the big Billy Goat Gruff, and he butted the troll into the river! Then he joined his brothers on the hill, and they all ate the sweet grass.

The Endless Tale

Many years ago in the Far East, there was a great king who loved stories.

He said, "The man that can tell me a never-ending story will marry my daughter, and shall be king after me."

The king's daughter was very pretty and many men tried to fulfill the task, but all their stories eventually came to an end. Then one day a stranger from the south came into the palace and said, "I have a pleasant story about locusts, which I would like to tell."

"Do tell it," said the king. "I will gladly listen."

The storyteller began his tale.

"Once upon a time, a king stored all the corn in his country in a strong granary. But a swarm of hungry locusts came and saw where the grain had been put. They found a teeny-tiny crack that was just large enough for one locust to pass through at a time. So one locust went in and carried away a grain of corn, then another locust went in and carried away a grain of corn, then another locust went in and carried away a grain of corn..."

Day after day, week after week,
the man kept on saying, "Then
another locust went in and carried
away a grain of corn..."
A month passed, a year
passed, and at the end of two
years, the king said, "How much
longer will the locusts be going in
and carrying away corn?"
"Oh King," said the storyteller,
"they have not yet cleared one
cubit, and there are many
thousands of cubits in the
granary."
"Man, man," cried the
king, "I can listen to it no
longer. Take my daughter, be
my heir, rule my kingdom.
But do not let me hear
another word about those
horrible locusts!"

Eat, My Clothes!

A peasant boy called Giufà was invited to a wedding, so he put on his only coat, which was very ragged, and set off. The family, when they saw him looking so poor, came near to setting the dogs on him, and offered him no food or drink.

When his mother heard about it, she scrimped and saved and bought him a fine coat, a pair of breeches, and a velvet waistcoat.

At the next wedding he was invited to, Giufà wore his new clothes. This time he was invited to eat with the family. Everyone was very polite to him. Giufà filled his stomach, and then starting putting food into his pockets, coat, and hat saying, "Eat, my clothes, for you are welcome, not I!"

The Bear and the Fox
Go into Partnership

The fox called Reynard and the bear called Bruin made up their minds to share a field so that they could grow their own crops. The first year they sowed wheat. "Now we must share and share alike," said Reynard, the fox. "You can have the roots and I will have the tops."

So when they had threshed the crop, the fox got all the grain, while Bruin got nothing but the muddy roots. Bruin didn't like this, but Reynard said it was what they had agreed. "Another year it will be your turn. You can then have the tops, and I will be satisfied with the roots."

Bruin was happy with that. But next spring the crafty Reynard sowed carrots in the field. When autumn came Reynard took the carrots, but Bruin only got the leafy tops.

Bruin realized Reynard had tricked him once more — and the angry bear never spoke to the cunning fox again!

The Husband of the Rat's Daughter

A rat and his wife had one daughter, the loveliest girl in the rat world.

As she grew up, her parents began to look for a suitable husband. Her mother declared, "My daughter shall never marry a mere rat."

"We had better offer her in marriage to the Sun," answered her husband. "There is nothing greater."

So the next morning, the three rats set out to see the Sun.

At length they came to the golden palace where the Sun lived. But when they offered him their daughter, he said, "There is something greater than I am, and that is the cloud, for he can cover me." So the mother repeated her proposal to the cloud.

"Alas," said the cloud, "the wind is more powerful than I, for he can push me around the sky."

So, turning to the wind, the mother began her little speech once more.

"The wall is the proper husband for your daughter," answered the wind, "for he has the power to stop me in my flight."

Then something happened that was quite unexpected. The rat daughter burst into tears. "I won't marry that ugly old wall," she sobbed. "I would have married the others, because it was my duty, although I love a handsome young rat, and him only. But the wall – no!"

And the wall declared, "It is quite true that I can stop the wind, who can part the clouds, who can cover the sun – but there is someone more powerful than I, and that is the rat. The rat can reduce me to powder, simply with his teeth. If you want a son-in-law who is greater than the whole world, seek him among the rats."

So all three returned home, and the rat's daughter happily married her handsome young rat.

The King o' the Cats

The gravedigger's wife was sitting with her big black cat, Old Tom, when her husband arrived home one evening. "Oh, I have such a strange tale to tell you. I was digging away when I heard a cat's meow and what do you think I saw?"

"What?"

"Nine black cats. They were carrying a small coffin covered with black velvet, and at every third step they cried all together, 'Meow—'

"Meow!" said Old Tom.

"Then they all stopped and looked at me. One came forwards and said to me – yes, said to me – 'Tell Tom Tildrum that Tim Toldrum's dead.'"

At this, Old Tom yelled, "What – old Tim dead! Then I'm the King o' the Cats!" And he rushed up the chimney and was never seen again.

The Star Money

Long ago, there was a young orphan girl who was so poor that she had nowhere to live. One cold day on her travels, she met a starving beggar. He looked so hungry that she gave him her last piece of bread.

A few miles further on she came across a shivering boy. She took off her jacket and wrapped it around him.

Further on, she saw a beggar girl, stick-thin and wearing rags. The little orphan gave away her own dress to warm her. Next she came to another poor child, whose feet were bare and bleeding. The girl gave her shoes to the boy.

The orphan girl now had nothing, but she still travelled on. As she walked, she gazed up at the millions of stars in the night sky. They glittered and began to fall — there were coins falling all around her! The girl hurried to gather as many as she could. Soon she had enough to never want for anything ever again — and she lived happily ever after.

How the Goblins Turned to Stone

Goblins of Holland live deep underground, as daylight turns them to stone. They only come out at night, then cause trouble and mischief, wearing red caps, which make them invisible.

One day, a little Dutch girl called Alida found a goblin cap, and she left a note telling the owner to come to a field that night with all the other goblins to fetch it back. Then she gathered hundreds of men together in the dark. She told them to feel for the goblins, snatch their hats off and then hold them until daylight came. The goblins arrived and the men began to grab, snatch and pull. In a few minutes, hundreds of red caps were in their hands and many wriggling goblins became visible. The men held the goblins firmly and at the first ray of the sun, they all turned to stone. The stones can still be seen in Holland today.

The Farmer with the Small Barn

A **farmer had a barn** so small that it only just had room for his cow. He was content, but his wife begged him to buy a donkey as well, for her to ride. The farmer knew this donkey would not leave his cow enough space, but in the end he gave in and bought a donkey.

This made the barn very crowded – the two animals kept jostling each other. In the end, the farmer prayed to God to let the cow die. "That way," he said, "my wife won't blame me and the donkey will be comfortable."

The next morning, when the farmer entered the barn his poor donkey had died.

"Dear Lord," he complained, "with all your wisdom, can't you tell the difference between a donkey and a cow?"

The Little Mermaid

Once upon a time, a Sea King lived deep under the ocean with his daughter, the little mermaid. One day the little mermaid was playing at the surface when she saw a ship. In it was a handsome young prince. She stayed and watched the ship until it grew late but then a storm arose and the ship sank!

The little mermaid swam desperately to find the prince, rescued him, and took him to the shore. She was sad, because she knew they couldn't live together, even though she loved him. 'I will see if the sea witch can help me,' she thought. She left the prince, and swam to the sea witch's lair.

The sea witch thought for a time, then said, "I can give you legs. But every step will feel like treading on knives. If the prince marries you, you will become human. But if he marries another, you will become foam on the waves."

"I'll do it," said the brave little mermaid.

"But I must be paid," said the witch. "You have the sweetest voice under the waves. Give it to me."

"So be it," the little mermaid whispered. The witch took her voice and gave her a potion. The little mermaid drank it even though it felt as if she were swallowing fire, and she fainted.

When the sun rose, the mermaid was lying on the sand and before her stood the handsome young prince, smiling. She had legs and feet, and she was wearing clothes!

The prince asked who she was, but she could not speak. He helped her to stand and walk, and every step she took was painful, but she didn't mind because she was with him.

The prince took her back to his palace. He was charmed by her and said she would stay with him always. But one morning, the little mermaid woke to the sound of church bells.

"Today is my wedding day," the prince explained to her. "My father has ordered that I get married."

The wedding was held and the little mermaid was a bridesmaid. But her mind was filled with the thought of becoming foam on the waves.

The wedding party continued late into the night, but the little mermaid was so sad that she decided to leave, and await her fate on the shore. As the first ray of dawn lit the sky, the little mermaid threw herself into the sea — but her body did not dissolve into foam. All around her floated beautiful transparent beings. "We are spirits," one of the beings explained. "We fly around the world doing good deeds. You have been chosen to join us, as you gave up everything for love."

The little mermaid's heart was filled with joy at last, and she flew away with the spirits to be happy forever.

The Farmers and the Storm

A **group of men** were working in a field one day when a terrible storm broke out. Lightning flashed and thunder crashed. They all rushed to a barn and hid inside, but the storm still raged.

"The gods are angry with one of us," the men decided. "Let us put all our hats outside and see which one draws the lightning."

They did so and lightning struck the straw hat of one poor fellow. Seeing this, the others pushed him out into the storm, saying, "We can't help you — go and receive your punishment."

Not wanting his friends to suffer with him, the man agreed to go. As he stood there trembling, the lightning struck the barn instead — so only the good man was left unhurt.

The Morning and the Evening Star

Once upon a time there were two stars. One was named Tschen and the other Shen. Both were sons of the Golden King of the Heavens. One day they quarrelled, and Tschen struck Shen a terrible blow. Afterwards both stars made a vow that they would never again look upon each other, and to this day Tschen only appears in the evening, and Shen only appears in the morning. Tschen and Shen are also known as Hesperus and Lucifer, the morning and evening stars.

And that is why people say, "When two brothers do not live peaceably with one another they are like Tschen and Shen."

Jupiter and the Monkey

Long ago the great god Jupiter, who ruled over the Earth, issued a proclamation to all the beasts. He offered a prize to the one who, in his judgement, produced the most beautiful child.

All the animals were so proud of their children that they were sure they would win the prize. They came in herds and flocks and swarms to make an enormous queue before Jupiter to show him their babies. Among them came the monkey, carrying her baby in her arms. It was a hairless, flat-nosed little thing, and when the gods saw it, they burst into laughter. However, the monkey hugged her baby and said, "Jupiter may give the prize to whoever he likes, but I shall always think my baby the most beautiful."

Beauty is in the eye of the beholder.

The Water Nix

Many years ago, a brother and sister were playing by a well when the girl toppled in! Her brother reached out to save her, but he fell in too! Unfortunately, a mischievous water sprite called a nix lived down below. She grabbed them, saying, "Got you! Now you will live with me and do all my hard work."

The little boy had to chop down trees for firewood and the little girl had to spin at a spinning wheel. They both had to fetch water, but their buckets had holes.

After several weeks a chance came for them to escape. The water nix went out and as soon as she was gone the two children set off. When the nix found her servants gone, she was furious! She ran off after them with huge strides. The little boy and girl looked behind them. The water nix was coming!

Quick as lightning, the little girl took her hairbrush from her pocket and threw it behind her. While the children kept running, the hairbrush grew and grew — until it was a hill covered in sharp spikes that blocked the water nix's path.

The water nix roared with rage but she picked her way through slowly. Soon she was gaining on them again, so the little girl threw her pocket mirror behind her as far as she could. While the children kept running, the mirror grew and grew — until it was a mountain made entirely of glass. It was so slippery that it was impossible for the nix to cross it no matter how much she chopped at it with her axe! How the nix gnashed her teeth!

At last the little boy and girl found their way back home. And there they lived happily ever after — unlike the water nix, who had only her wicked self for company.

Little Tuck

There was once a young boy called Tuck. One day, he had a geography test to revise for, but his mother kept him busy with jobs all day. He cooked and cleaned, looked after his sister, and even helped an old washerwoman with her washing.

By the time he had finished however, dusk was falling and it was too dim inside the cottage to read – all Tuck could do was go to bed. He put his geography book under his pillow, because he had heard one of his friends say that if you did, the information sank into your brain while you slept.

Tuck didn't realise that the washerwoman he'd helped knew magic. She rewarded his kindness by sending him a vivid dream, in which he met animals from all over the world. They told him all about their countries and the names of the capital cities so that when Tuck awoke the following morning, he knew everything that came up on his test!

The Wolf and the Shepherd

A shepherd was out on the hillside one morning when he found a tiny wolf cub. He decided to take the poor thing home.

The shepherd reared the cub with his dogs, training it to herd the sheep. When the cub grew to his full size, if ever a wolf stole a sheep from the flock, it would join the dogs in hunting it down. But if the dogs failed to find the thief, the wolf would continue the hunt alone, and when it found the culprit, would stop and share the feast. As well as this, if some time passed without a sheep being carried off by the wolves, it would steal one for itself.

Eventually, the shepherd became suspicious. He kept a close watch on the wolf, until he caught it in the act of stealing a sheep. And that was the end of the ungrateful creature.

What's bred in the bone is sure to come out in the flesh.

Momotaro

A woman who had no children found a baby boy in a peach, so she brought him up as her own. She called him Momotaro, which means 'son of a peach'.

When Momotaro was seventeen he went to visit an island where an ogre lived, to try to steal his fortune. He had not gone far when he met a wasp.

"Give me a share of your food, Momotaro," said the wasp, "and I will help you overcome the ogre."

"Yes of course," said Momotaro.

Soon after he met a crab, and the same agreement was made, and then with a chestnut, and last of all with a millstone.

When they reached the island they found the ogre's house but the ogre was nowhere to be found, so they made a plan. The chestnut laid itself down in the ash of a charcoal fire that had been burning on the hearth, the crab hid himself in a washing pan nearly full of water, the wasp settled in a dusky corner, the millstone climbed onto the roof, and Momotaro hid in the garden.

Before long the ogre came back, and he went to the fire to warm himself. The chestnut threw burning cinders over the ogre's hands. The ogre at once ran to the washing pan, to cool his burns, and the crab caught his fingers and pinched them. Snatching his hands out of the pan, the ogre leapt into the corner where the wasp stung him dreadfully.

In a great fright the ogre tried to run out of the room, but down came the millstone with a crash on his head and killed him at once.

So, with the help of his faithful friends, which he had made through his kindness, Momotaro got all the ogre's gold and his fortune was made.

The Stone Soup

Many years ago, three soldiers walked into a village. They begged for food but the poor villagers said that no one had anything to spare. The first soldier said to the villagers, "Very well then. We will teach you how to make soup from stones."

They put a pot on a fire and dropped in three stones. "This will be a fine soup," the second soldier said, "but a pinch of salt and some parsley would make it wonderful!"

Up jumped a villager, returning with parsley, salt and also a turnip.

Soon villagers had also donated barley, carrots, beef and cream and everyone was sitting down to eat the delicious soup. They thanked the soldiers for teaching them their secret. The third soldier turned to the crowd, and said, "There is no secret — it is only by sharing that we may make a feast."

The Father and his Daughters

A man once had two daughters, one of whom grew up to marry a gardener, while the other daughter married a potter.

After a time, the man went to visit his daughters. First, he went to the gardener's wife. He asked her how things were going. She replied, "I wish we could have some heavy rain. All our fruit and vegetables are about to wither and die."

Then the man went to the potter's wife. She said, "I wish we could have some dry weather, to dry the pottery." Her father looked at her. "You want dry weather," he said, "and your sister wants rain. I was going to ask in my prayers that your wishes be granted, but now it strikes me I had better not refer to the subject."

You can't please everybody.

The Buckwheat

Long ago, there was a field of buckwheat. The buckwheat did not bend in the wind like other grains, instead, they stood up straight and stiff, holding their heads up proudly.

One night, a terrible storm came and all the plants in the cornfields folded their leaves and bowed their heads to avoid harm. But the buckwheat stood up straighter than ever.

"Bow down," urged the old willow tree.

"Nothing can make us bow down," said the buckwheat. And boldly the buckwheat looked straight up, while lightning blazed across the sky.

When the storm had died away, the wildflowers raised their heads. They felt quite refreshed by the rain. However, the buckwheat was a sorry sight. They were scorched black by the lightning and lay across the earth, defeated after all.

The Shipwrecked Man and the Sea

A man who had been shipwrecked was struggling for his life in the sea. He was about to give up when finally he was washed up on a beach, and at once fell into a deep sleep.

When the man awoke, he was furious, and he raged at the sea, which was now completely smooth. "How deceitful you are!" he cried. "You draw people in by showing your peaceful side, but when you have us in your power, you become cruel and punish us."

To his huge surprise, the sea then appeared in the form of a woman, and replied, "Don't blame me, O sailor, it's the fault of the winds. By nature I am calm and safe, but the winds buffet me with their gusts and gales, and whip me into a monster."

Be sure you're blaming the right person.

The Troll who Wrote a Letter

A troll had just built his house on a riverbank when the people of the nearby town, which was called Kund, built a church right next to it. This made him cross as all trolls hate the sound of bells ringing.

The troll decided to leave, and made his new home in a swamp instead, but he continued to hate the people for forcing him out of his old home.

Not long after, a man walked past the swamp and met the old troll on the road. "Where do you live?" asked the troll.

The man answered, "I am from Kund."

The troll had been waiting for a chance like this to get his revenge. "Ah," he said, "Will you be so kind as to take a letter from me, back with you to Kund?"

The man said he would gladly do so. The troll took a letter out of his pocket and said,"I beg you then, to take this letter to Kund. And when you get there, throw it over the churchyard wall."

'What a strange way to deliver a letter,' thought the man. He walked on a little way, but he felt a great curiosity to look at the letter.

'I won't open it,' he thought, 'I'll just look at it.' So he took the letter out of his pocket. At once a little water began to dribble out. Then the letter unfolded itself and the water came pouring in such great waves that the poor man had to scramble for his life!

The wicked troll, hoping to drown the church, had enclosed a whole lake in the letter, but luckily the lake ran out into a meadow instead!

Nasreddin Hodja and the Naughty Boy

One day Nasreddin Hodja bought a donkey. He started to walk home, leading it behind him, when two boys decided to trick him.

One of them snuck up behind Nasreddin, loosened the halter and put it around his own neck. The other boy took the donkey away to sell.

When they reached home, Nasreddin Hodja saw the boy.

"Who are you?" he said.

"I misbehaved and made my mother miserable. She put a curse on me and I turned into a donkey. When you bought me, the curse ended."

"I will let you go, but never again torment your mother," said Nasreddin.

The next day Nasreddin Hodja went looking for a donkey to buy. He saw the donkey he'd bought the day before. He went up to it and whispered, "You naughty boy! You disobeyed your mother again, didn't you?"

Foolish Hans
Saves a Man

A man had climbed a tree to pick some apples and couldn't get down again.

"Help me!" he called out to some passers-by. Foolish Hans happened to be among them and announced that he would save the man. He took a long rope and threw it up to the man in the tree, telling him to tie it around his waist. "How will this help?" the people asked.

"Trust me," Hans said, "I saved a man like this once before."

The man did as he was told, Hans gave a strong tug and pulled the man out of the tree. He fell to the ground with a bump and was quite hurt.

Hans scratched his head thoughtfully, "Now I come to think of it," he said, "the last man I saved was in a river."

The Ogre's Bride

Molly was about to be married to an ogre. Her father had promised the match, but as she didn't want the ogre for a husband she decided to find a way out of it.

When the ogre came to her father's house to talk about the wedding she cooked a fine stew. "What a delicious meal!" said the ogre.

"Made with dead rats!" lied Molly.

'How I will save money when I marry her,' thought the ogre. "When can we marry?" he asked.

"Only once you've built me a house and made me a bed stuffed with feathers from the sky," said Molly. The ogre agreed, and soon built her a farmhouse.

The very day it was complete there was a snowstorm, and Molly sent for the ogre. "Now you see the feathers falling," she said, pointing at the snow, "use them to fill the bed."

The ogre carried in shovelfuls of snow but it melted as fast as he put it in. Towards night the room got so cold that the snow stopped melting and the bed was soon filled. Molly came to inspect the ogre's work, and said, "Very good. Rest here tonight. Tomorrow we will be married."

So the tired ogre lay down on the bed he had filled with snow, but he could not get warm. In the morning he woke with such horrible pains in his bones that he could hardly move. "It's no use," he groaned, "to sleep on such a bed would be the death of me." And he went off home as quickly as he could, before Molly could arrive to be married.

It is said that the ogre never recovered and was less powerful than before. As for Molly, with a new fine farmhouse she had lots of offers of marriage, and lived happily ever after.

The Donkey, the Fox and the Lion

There was once a donkey and a fox who set out to look for something to eat, but they hadn't gone far when they saw a lion coming their way. The donkey looked around for a place to hide, while the fox thought he saw a way of saving himself.

He approached the lion and whispered, "If you let me go, I will help you get the donkey." The lion agreed. The fox then returned to the donkey. He told him that he had found a hiding place, but instead led the donkey over a pit that a hunter had dug as a trap. The donkey fell down into it. But the lion immediately pounced on the fox and gobbled him up. Then he had plenty of time to eat the donkey.

If you betray a friend, you should expect to be betrayed yourself.

The Fawn and his Mother

A **female deer** had a baby fawn which she cared for very well. The fawn grew to be big and strong. However he seemed to be afraid of everything he came across, and jumped easily.

One day, the mother deer looked at her son and said, "My boy, nature has given you a powerful body and a stout pair of antlers. You could charge at anything with those and run them right through! Why do you run away from everything?"

Just then they both heard the sound of a pack of hounds in full cry — they knew that huntsmen must be coming. And with that, they both ran off as fast as their legs could carry them.

A coward by nature will always be a coward.

MAY

The Cunning Rat

A rat was just about to come out of his hole when he caught a glimpse of a cat waiting for him. He went down to the tunnels at the bottom of his hole, and invited a friend to join him in a visit to a neighbouring corn-bin. "I would have gone alone," he said, "but it's always nicer with two."

"Very well," said the friend, "I will go with you. Lead on."

"Lead?" exclaimed the other. "No, indeed – after you, sir, after you."

Pleased with this politeness, the friend went ahead, and leaving the hole first, immediately had to run for his life as the cat made a pounce at him. The other rat scampered out safely after!

The Iron Stove

A **princess was once walking** in a forest when she found an iron stove. Out of the stove came a voice crying, "Help me! I am an enchanted prince. I beg you to free me. If you can help, I shall make you my queen!"

"I will," promised the princess.

She took a knife from her bag and scraped a hole in the stove until it was large enough for the prince to climb out. "I thank you with all my heart," the prince said, before asking the princess to marry him, and travel to his kingdom. She said yes!

First though, she wanted to say goodbye to her father. "Very well," agreed the prince, "but you mustn't speak more than three words."

Of course, the princess forgot her promise and spoke more than three words as she told her father about the prince. A magic wind wiped every memory of her from the prince's head, and it carried him back to his own kingdom.

The princess searched for the prince for days but there was no sign of him. Finally, she stumbled across a little cottage. She went inside and found a toad who asked if he could help her. The princess told the toad everything, and when she had finished it gave her a nut, which she could open if she needed help, and a map to the prince's kingdom. She had to cross a high glass mountain, a field with plants as sharp as swords, and a lake as wide as the sea.

When the princess finally reached her sweetheart's castle her clothes were ragged and tattered and she wasn't allowed in. Suddenly, the princess remembered the nut. She cracked it open and inside was a beautiful gown. She put it on and as soon as the prince saw her he remembered her. They were soon married and lived happily ever after!

The Fierce Lion and the Cunning Little Jackal

In the jungle there lived a great lion. He killed and ate all the other animals until one day there were only a few left. The little jackal was scared he would be next, so he made a plan.

He went to the lion's den and said to the lion, "I'm so frightened! There is another lion in the jungle who is even more fierce than you."

"What!" roared the lion, "Lead me to him."

Then the little jackal led the lion to a deep well, and, pointing down to the lion's own reflection in the water, said, "He's down there!"

At once the lion jumped in to kill his deadly foe, but nothing was there — only his reflection.

Try as he might, the lion could not climb out of the well — he may still be there now. And the clever little jackal is safe.

The Swan
and the Goose

There was a rich man who bought a goose and a swan. He fed the goose well, planning to cook it for a feast one day. He enjoyed listening to the swan's beautiful song, however, so he decided to keep it as a pet.

The time finally arrived for the man to hold his feast. His cook made many delicious dishes, then went to catch the goose for cooking. But it was so dark outside that the cook could hardly tell one bird from the other and by mistake he caught the swan instead of the goose. The swan, knowing it was about to be killed, burst into one last beautiful song. Of course then the cook realized that he had the wrong bird – and so the swan was saved by its singing.

Sweet words may save us from danger when harsh words fail.

The Twelve Huntsmen

A prince and princess were once very deeply in love, but the prince's dying father had made his son promise to marry someone else. When the princess heard this, she cried as if she would never stop. "How can I help you feel better?" begged her father. The princess thought hard and said, "Father, please find eleven girls exactly like me."

He searched high and low and eventually found eleven girls just like his daughter. Then the princess asked for twelve suits of huntsmen's clothes to be made and she and the eleven girls put them on. Then they all set off on horseback to her sweetheart's castle, for he was now king. She asked him to hire them as huntsmen and the new king did so, although he didn't recognize his love.

The next day, the king called for his new huntsmen to lead him on a hunt through the forest. As they were riding, a messenger arrived with news that the king's bride-to-be would be arriving at the castle that day.

When the princess heard this, she fell to the ground in a faint. The king raced at once to her, thinking that the brave captain of his huntsmen was ill. He leant over her, taking off her hat and gloves but when he saw the face of his princess and recognized his ring on her finger, he gasped in joy.

"Forgive me, father," he murmured, "but I cannot marry the other princess."

Then he kissed her and told her, "You are mine, and I am yours."

The king sent a messenger to explain to the other princess that he was very sorry but he could no longer marry her. As luck would have it she wasn't disappointed as she had fallen in love with the king's friend, a duke. And so two weddings were celebrated – and they were all very happy indeed.

The Butterfly

There was once a butterfly who wanted to fall in love. He didn't want a butterfly for a wife though – he wanted to marry a flower. The problem was, he couldn't decide which was the prettiest.

He flew to the violets, but he thought their scent was too strong. He flew to the tulips, but their colours were too bright. One day while still in search of the perfect bloom, the butterfly flew in through a window. The people in the room caught him and pinned him to a piece of cardboard. "Now I'm sitting on a stalk, just like the flowers," the butterfly sighed. "And it isn't fun."

Too late, he realized he had been mistaken all along. "Beauty just isn't enough to make you happy," he sighed. "To be happy, you must have freedom and sunshine."

The Mice and the Weasels

The mice and the weasels fought many battles, but the mice always lost. At last the mice called a meeting to discuss tactics. One old mouse got up to speak.

"We need generals to plan our battles and direct the movements of our troops."

This made a lot of sense to the other mice and they at once chose the biggest among them to be their generals.

The generals put on big helmets decorated with plumes of straw, then led the mice to battle. However, they were defeated as usual and soon all the mice were scampering back to their holes. They all reached safety, except the generals. They couldn't squeeze into their holes because their helmets were too big — and they were left to the clutches of the weasels.

Greatness carries its own dangers and punishments.

The Husband who was to Mind the House

Once upon a time there was a man who thought his wife never did anything right in the house. "Well," said his wife, "tomorrow let's change jobs. I'll go out to the fields, and you can mind the house."

So the next morning the wife went out with her husband's scythe, and the man began to do the work at home. First of all he wanted to churn the butter to make cream, but when he had churned for a while, he got thirsty, and went down to the cellar to tap a barrel of ale. He had just started when he heard a commotion in the kitchen above. The man ran up the cellar steps, and when he got there he

found the pig rolling in the cream, which it had upset onto the floor. By the time he had put the pig out and returned to the cellar, all the ale had run out of the barrel.

The man was mopping the cellar floor when all of a sudden he remembered that the cow hadn't had a bite to eat all morning. He decided it was too far to take the cow to the meadow, so he came up with a plan and pulled her onto the roof, for it was an earth roof, and a fine crop of grass was growing there. Worried that the cow might fall off the roof, he tied one end of a rope to the cow's leg and slipped the other end down the chimney and tied it around his own leg.

The man was just feeling very pleased with himself when the cow fell off the roof, dragging the man up the chimney! There he stuck with the cow hanging halfway down the wall outside.

When this wife got home and saw the cow hanging there, she cut the rope with her scythe. As she did this, her husband fell down from within the chimney. She found him upside down with his head in the porridge pot and he never said a word against her again.

Nasreddin Hodja Rescues the Moon

One evening Nasreddin Hodja went to the well to draw some water. There he saw the moon's reflection. Thinking it had fallen into the well, he said, "I will have to pull it out immediately." He took a rope with a hook fastened to one end and lowered it into the well.

The hook caught on a rock, and he called, "I have it!" but then the rope broke, causing the Hodja to fall onto his back. Lying there he saw the moon in the sky and cried out, "I have hurt myself, but at least the moon is back where it belongs!"

The Sorcerer's Apprentice

A sorcerer left his workshop to visit a friend, leaving his young apprentice with water to carry and cleaning to do. After a while, the apprentice grew bored of the hard work and looked into the sorcerer's magic book to try and find a spell to help him. He enchanted a broom to sweep and carry water, and for a while it worked. But the broom brought bucket after bucket of water until the floor was awash.

The apprentice then realized he didn't know how to stop the spell! He seized an axe and cut the broom in half, but that made two brooms that worked even faster. Soon there was so much water that the apprentice was nearly swimming! Just in time, the old sorcerer came back and broke the spell. And luckily for the apprentice he forgave his pupil for interfering.

The Trumpeter Taken Prisoner

Once there was a brave army trumpeter who strayed too close to the enemy and was captured. The soldiers were about to put him to death, when the young trumpeter begged for mercy.

"Look at me — I am not a fighter," he said. "I don't even carry a weapon. All I do is blow this trumpet — and how can that hurt you? So please spare my life, I have done nothing to you."

But the enemy soldiers answered grimly, "By sounding out the orders, you guide and encourage your soldiers in battle. They and you have killed hundreds of our men, so now you must pay the price for your music."

Those who stir up trouble are as guilty as those who carry it.

The Fool in India

A **foolish man** was once travelling from one village to another in India, but lost his way. When he asked for help, the people said to him, "When you get to the riverbank, take the path that goes up by the tree."

The fool reached the river and thinking that he was following their instructions, climbed up the great tree that stood on its bank. The bough at the end bent with his weight, and it was all he could do to avoid falling into the river.

While he was clinging to it, there came along an elephant and its driver on his back. The fool called to the driver, saying,

"Please, help! I can't get down."

The elephant-driver took hold of the fool's feet with both his hands, but his elephant carried on walking! The driver found himself clinging to the feet of the fool, who was clinging to the end of the tree.

Then the fool said to the driver, "Sing something loudly, so that the people hear us, and come and help."

So the elephant-driver began to sing, and he sang so sweetly that the fool was delighted, and forgetting where he was, let go of the tree so he could applaud. Immediately he and the driver fell into the river with a splash!

The Hare and the Tortoise

A **hare was once boasting** to the other animals about how speedy he was. To prove it he asked the tortoise to race him.

"Ready, set, go!" bellowed the ox.

The hare darted out of sight. As soon as he rounded the bend, he thought he'd have a laugh at the tortoise's expense. He lay down under a tree and pretended to nap – just to show that he could stop to sleep and still beat the tortoise. But it was so cool and peaceful in the shade that the hare fell asleep!

Slowly, slowly, the tortoise plodded on – past the sleeping hare – until the finish line was in sight. All at once the hare woke with a start. He saw the tortoise ahead and bounded after him, but the tortoise passed the finish line before he could catch up!

Slow and steady wins the race.

The Money Pig

In the playroom, lots of toys were lying about. There were teddy bears and building blocks, drawing pencils and toy soldiers, a dolls' house and a train set. High up on top of a cupboard was a china money box, in the shape of a pig. It was stuffed full of coins.

The money pig was very proud of itself. It knew very well that what it had in its stomach would have bought all the other toys — and they knew it too.

One night, one of the dolls suggested excitedly, "Shall we play a game of Men and Women?"

All the toys jumped up and down in excitement shouting, "Yes! Yes! Let's!"

"I haven't decided if I will join in," the money pig sniffed. "But one thing's for sure —

I shall stay up here in my high position and you will have to involve me in the game like that."

"Very well," said the toys, eager to begin.

Thoughtfully, they pushed and dragged the toy theatre in front of the cupboard so the money pig could see directly in. Then they all took turns on the stage, acting out different men and women having afternoon tea together. That was what they called 'playing Men and Women'.

In fact, it would have been better if the pig had climbed down and joined in with the game because all of a sudden – *BAM!* – someone bumped into the cupboard. The money pig toppled off and was smashed to pieces on the ground. Next day, the family swept up all the broken bits of the proud money pig and put them in the bin. By afternoon, a brand new money pig was standing on top of the cupboard – its tummy completely empty.

The Frog
and the Snail

A frog entered into a bet with a snail as to which of them would be the first to reach the city. The frog, of course, believed that he would win because he could travel so much faster than the snail.

As they started out the frog made fun of the snail: "Don't crawl along so. Instead hop like I do, otherwise you'll never win." Then away he hopped. However, arriving at the city, he found that the city gate was closed, so he had to wait until morning when the gate would be opened.

In the meantime the snail crawled steadily onward, and she too finally arrived at the city. Of course, she also found the gate closed, but for her that was no problem. She simply crawled up and over it, and thus won the bet.

The Four Oxen and the Lion

Once upon a time there were four oxen who lived in a field. A lion regularly used to prowl around, wondering how he could catch one of them to eat. Many a time the lion tried to attack the oxen, but whenever he came near, they all stood with their tails together. In this way, from whichever direction the lion approached, he was met by the horns of one of the oxen – and very long, sharp horns they were too.

One day, however, the oxen argued among themselves and each stomped off to a different corner of the field to graze. The lion found them like that and sprang to attack. No sooner had one fallen than he took down the second, the third, and then the last.

United we stand, divided we fall.

The Lion, the Goat and the Baboon

The lion and the goat were once happily married and they had lots of little baby goats.

One day, when the goat went to market, a baboon knocked on the door. The polite lion kindly invited him into his house to meet his children.

The baboon looked at the little goats and said, "Why, they look very tasty, you know."

The lion didn't know what to do. The little goats ran and hid, for the baboon was much bigger than them, with long sharp teeth.

Mother goat arrived home soon after, and the lion quietly warned her of their guest's words. She thought for a minute then fetched some molasses. The lion tasted it, and said, "It's very good, what is it?"

The goat answered loudly, "It's baboon's blood."

At this the baboon rushed off and never came near them again.

The Two Travellers
and the Farmer

A traveller came upon a farmer hoeing in his field. "What sort of people live in the next town?" the traveller asked.

"What were the people like where you're from?" replied the farmer.

"Selfish, lazy, stupid, and not one of them to be trusted. I'm happy to be leaving."

"Is that so?" replied the old farmer. "Well, I'm afraid that you'll find the same sort in the next town.

Sometime later another stranger, coming from the same direction stopped to talk. "What sort of people live in the next town?" he asked.

"What were the people like where you've come from?" replied the farmer once again.

"The best people in the world. Hardworking, honest, and friendly. I'm sorry to be leaving them."

"Don't worry," said the farmer. "You'll find the same sort in the next town."

The Frog Prince

Long ago, there lived a king who had three daughters. Everyone agreed that the youngest princess was loveliest of all.

One hot day, the youngest princess lost her golden ball in a well. She sank down onto the mossy ground and started to cry.

"Don't cry," said a croaky voice. "I can get your ball back."

The princess looked up, startled. "Just promise," said the frog, "that we will be best friends. I want to eat off your golden plates, and sleep in your bed."

"Yes, yes," agreed the princess hurriedly.

The frog jumped into the well and reappeared holding the golden ball. The princess was delighted but forgot all about her promise and ran off. That evening, at the palace there was a knocking at the door and a voice croaked, "Let me in!"

The princess grew pale. She told her father what had happened.

The king looked grave. "You made a promise and you must keep it," he said firmly.

So the youngest princess let the frog in.

"Lift me up so I can sit and eat with you off your golden plates," the frog croaked.

When the frog's tummy was full, he gave a yawn.

"Delicious," he said. "Now let's sleep."

The princess carried him upstairs to her bedroom. She threw back the quilt and tucked the frog into the bed. Then something very strange happened. The frog transformed into a handsome prince. The prince explained how a wicked witch had enchanted him. The princess was the only one who could save him and, by carrying out her promise, she had broken the spell.

The prince and princess fell in love, and it wasn't long before they set off to the prince's kingdom in a golden carriage drawn by eight white horses. There they married and lived happily ever after.

Look Where
You Lost It

One summer evening, the front garden of the coffee house was well lit by the gas lamps placed on the few wooden tables. Nasreddin Hodja was, however, troubled. He was searching for something on the ground.

"What are you looking for?" some people nearby asked.

"I lost a gold coin in that alley," he said.

The other customers were mystified, "Then why are you looking for it here? You should search the alley where you lost it!"

Nasreddin Hodja answered simply, "But it is dark over there and I can't see anything. Here it is nice and bright, so I will search here, where I can see better."

The Farmer and Fortune

A **farmer was digging in his field** one morning when to his amazement he dug up a pot of golden coins. Of course, he was overjoyed at his discovery. From then on, every day he went to pray at the shrine of the Goddess of the Earth to say thank you for his find. However, the Goddess of Fortune came to hear about this and was jealous.

She came to see the farmer and angrily demanded, "Why do you give the Goddess of Earth the credit for the gift that I gave to you? You have not once thought of thanking me for your good luck! However, should you be unlucky enough to lose what you have gained, I know very well that you would blame me, Fortune, for your bad luck."

Show gratitude where gratitude is due.

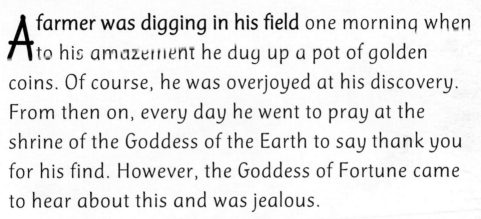

The Goose-girl

A queen had a beautiful daughter who was going to be married to a prince from a nearby kingdom. Arrangements were made for the princess to travel to his country, accompanied by her waiting-maid. The queen gave the princess a horse named Falada, which had the gift of speech.

However, when they stopped for the princess to drink from a stream, the waiting-maid forced the princess to swap clothes with her, then she climbed onto Falada's back. She told the princess she would kill her if she betrayed the secret, and they travelled on. When they arrived at the prince's kingdom the

king and prince greeted them. They took the maid to be the princess and led her into the palace, leaving the real one outside. The king said she could help Conrad, a servant, look after the geese.

Soon afterwards the disguised maid ordered that Falada should be beheaded so that it couldn't reveal her wicked deed. When the real princess heard the sad news, she persuaded them to mount Falada's head over the great gate through which she passed on her way to the goose pasture. The next morning, when she drove her geese under the gate, the princess cried:

"O Falada, hang you there?"

And the head replied to her:

"'Tis Falada, Princess fair.

If she knew this, for your sake

Your queen-mother's heart would break."

Conrad heard these strange words and decided he would tell the king that evening. Then they drove their geese onwards. As they neared the water meadows, the princess let down her long golden hair. Conrad thought it was beautiful — he wanted to pull out a strand for himself. But the princess called out, "Blow, blow, thou gentle wind. I say, blow Conrad's little hat away, and make him chase it here and there, until once more I have braided my hair." And there came such a strong gust of wind that Conrad's hat was blown far away, and he was forced to run after it.

That evening Conrad went to the king and told him about the speaking horse's head. The king questioned the princess afterwards, but she said very little. At last the king sighed and said, "If you will not tell your troubles to me, tell them to the iron stove." But as he left he hid, so he overheard what she said, "Here am I, doomed to be a goose-girl, while the false waiting-maid steals my bridegroom."

The king came back in and ordered her to be dressed in royal robes. She was so beautiful that he knew her to be the real princess. The wicked maid was banished from the kingdom at once, and the princess was married to the prince. They lived together happily ever after.

The Jackdaw and the Eagle

A jackdaw once saw a majestic eagle launch himself off a rock to seize a lamb and carry it off.

The jackdaw was full of admiration and decided to try the same thing. He dived upon a large ram but his claws became entangled in its fleece and he was not able to get himself free.

The shepherd laughed when he saw what had happened. Once he had cut the jackdaw free, he clipped his wings so he could no longer fly, then took him home and gave him to his children.

The children asked, "What sort of a bird is it?"

The shepherd replied, "It is a jackdaw, but it would like you to think it is an eagle."

If you pretend to be something you are not, prepare to be found out.

The Twelve Dancing Princesses

Once upon a time, there was a king who had twelve beautiful daughters. He could not understand one thing about them though — every morning, their shoes were worn through. The king announced that if anyone could discover what was going on, they could marry whichever princess they liked best. Many young men came to try their luck, but each time they fell asleep before finding out.

Then one day a soldier arrived in the kingdom and decided to find out what the princesses did each night. He took the advice of a wise old woman who told him not to drink anything the princesses gave him. She also gave him a cloak, and said, "When you wear this, you will be invisible."

The soldier set off for the castle. In the evening, he was shown into the princesses' bedroom and the king locked the door. One princess brought the soldier a goblet of wine but he didn't drink it. He then got into bed and pretended to sleep.

The twelve princesses then put on their finest dresses and climbed down through a trapdoor underneath one of the beds. Quickly, the soldier put on the cloak and followed them.

He came out into daylight, where he could see the princesses travelling in boats to an island. There was one boat left, and the soldier rowed after them, following the girls to a splendid castle. Inside, the great hall was decorated for a magnificent ball with glittering, golden trees. The soldier reached up to break off a twig to take with him.

SNAP! The youngest princess heard the noise and said to her sisters, "Do you think someone is here with us?"

The eldest said, "Of course not!"

The princesses joined the ball, and danced and danced for hours.

When their shoes were quite worn out, they started back home. The soldier raced ahead of them and lay back down in their bedroom, so they found him as they had left him — supposedly asleep.

The next morning he went to the king and told the tale of the trapdoor and the island, and how the princesses had danced all night. To prove it, he showed the king the golden twig. The king called for the princesses, who admitted the truth at once. The king told the soldier he could choose one girl for his wife. He chose the youngest princess and after they were married, he danced with her and her sisters every day.

The Beetle

The emperor's horse was a magnificent animal, with intelligent eyes and a mane like silk. The emperor ordered the royal blacksmith to make him four horseshoes out of pure gold – one for each hoof.

A tiny beetle living in the stable wanted gold shoes for his feet too, but the blacksmith only laughed at him. "Aren't I as good as the horse?" said the beetle, "And don't I belong to the emperor too?"

Then the beetle flew up to sit on the horse and said, "Now I'm the horse's rider and it's quite clear to me the horse was given golden shoes because of me, that's what I deserve – a horse with golden shoes!"

And to the beetle, the world was wonderful, because the emperor's favourite horse had golden shoes and because he was its rider.

The Donkey and the Wolf

A donkey was once grazing in a meadow when he caught sight of his enemy, the wolf, approaching. He knew he would be eaten unless he came up with a plan. So when the wolf reached him, the donkey said cunningly, "I have a thorn in my foot. Please would you pull it out? Otherwise, when you eat me, it might hurt you."

"How thoughtful of you," snarled the wolf. He told the donkey to lift up his foot, and set his mind to getting out the thorn. But the donkey suddenly kicked out with his heels and gave the wolf a blow to the mouth. Then he galloped off.

As soon as he was able, the wolf growled to himself, "It serves me right. My father taught me to kill, and I should have stuck to that instead of attempting to cure."

Stick to what you know and be true to yourself.

The Pointless Feast

One day a fox passed a lovely vineyard surrounded by a tall fence with a small hole in it. The fox could see what luscious grapes grew inside the vineyard, but the hole was too small for him to fit through. He ate nothing for three days until he became so thin that he managed to squeeze inside.

Inside the vineyard the fox began to eat. He grew bigger and fatter than ever before. Then he wanted to get out of the vineyard, but now the hole was too small again. So, as before, he ate nothing for three days, and just about managed to slip through the hole again.

Turning his head towards the vineyard, the poor fox said, "How pointless it was to eat that delicious fruit. I'm as thin as when I came in."

The Snail and the Rose Tree

Once upon a time, in a land far away, there was a beautiful garden. And in the middle of the garden a rose tree stood in full bloom. Under the blooming rose tree sat a tiny snail, thinking.

"Just wait," he muttered under his breath. "One day I will show everyone! I will do much better things than grow roses."

"How exciting!" replied the rose tree. "I can't wait to see what you will do. Can I ask when you are going to do it?"

"Well, as you may have noticed, I take my time," remarked the snail. "I mean, have you ever thought about why you bloom, and how it happens, and why it is that you bear roses and nothing else?"

"No," said the rose tree in a small voice. "I bloomed because I felt so glad about everything."

But then, a memory struck the rose tree. "I remember a little girl picking one rose and kissing it and giving it to her mother. Those times made me so happy! They were the best in my life."

And the rose tree went on blooming, while the snail lay lazily in his house, wanting nothing to do with the world.

Years rolled by and eventually the snail crumbled into the earth — and the rose tree too. In the garden, other rose trees bloomed, bringing happiness to many other people. And other snails crawled about, creeping into their houses and closing up the entrances tight, seeing nothing at all.

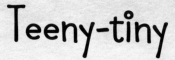

Teeny-tiny

Once upon a time there was a teeny-tiny old woman. She lived in a teeny-tiny house in a teeny-tiny street with a teeny-tiny cat. One day the teeny-tiny woman went for a teeny-tiny walk. She saw a teeny-tiny bone lying on top of a teeny-tiny grave. She put the teeny-tiny bone in her teeny-tiny pocket and went home to her teeny-tiny house. She was sitting in her teeny-tiny chair when she heard a teeny-tiny voice say, "Where is my teeny-tiny bone?"

The teeny-tiny woman sat up in her teeny-tiny chair and said in her teeny-tiny voice, "TAKE IT!"

And a teeny-tiny ghost ran out of the teeny-tiny house, down the teeny-tiny street into the teeny-tiny graveyard — with the teeny-tiny bone in its teeny-tiny hand!

The Nurse
and the Wolf

A nurse was once looking after a child who kept crying. "Be quiet now," she said, "or I'll give you to the wolf."

A wolf was passing under the window and heard the nurse saying this. So he crouched down by the house and waited.

'The child is sure to cry again soon,' he thought, 'then the nurse will throw it out for me.' So the wolf waited, until he heard the child crying again. The wolf sat under the window and looked up to the nurse, wagging his tail. But all the nurse did was gasp in horror and slam the window shut. She shrieked and the dogs of the house came bounding out, snarling.

Then the wolf realized that the nurse hadn't meant what she said, and he fled for his life.

Enemies' promises were made to be broken.

How the Dragon was Tricked

A young man once went to the king and asked to marry his daughter. The king said, "Bring me the covering from the bed of the great dragon, and I will think about it."

So the young man went away to the dragon's house and climbed up onto the roof. Then he let himself down through a window in the ceiling on a rope, and tried to hook the bed covering to draw it up. But the dragon woke and pulled the young man into the room!

He tied him up, roaring to his wife, "Tomorrow, kill him and cook him and we will eat him together."

The following morning the dragoness took hold of the young man, but as she untied the cords, he seized her and threw her into the oven. Then he snatched up the bed covering and carried it to the king.

"That is not enough," said the king. "Bring me

the dragon himself."

"It shall be done," answered the youth. So he disguised himself as a beggar and went again to the dragon's house. The young man found the dragon very busy making a box. "What is the box for?" he inquired.

"It is for the man who killed my wife, and stole my bed covering," said the dragon.

"He deserves nothing better," answered the beggar. "Still, that box doesn't look big enough."

"You are wrong," said the dragon tucking himself carefully inside the box. "The box is large enough even for me."

Quick as a flash, the young man clapped the lid on tight, and drove in nails to make it tighter still. Then he took the box on his back and brought it to the king, who finally let him marry his daughter.

JUNE

Androcles and the Lion

There was once a slave named Androcles who managed to escape his master, fleeing into the forest. There he discovered a lion groaning with pain. Androcles saw the lion's paw had a huge thorn stuck in it. He pulled out the thorn and the lion bowed its head to Androcles and licked his hand.

A few days later, Androcles was recaptured and condemned to fight with beasts in the Roman arena. He was led out and stood in terror as a lion was released and came bounding towards him. Suddenly the lion stopped. It looked at Androcles and then licked his hands. It was the lion from the forest!

Everyone was amazed, and the emperor summoned Androcles, who told his story. The emperor pardoned Androcles and let him and the lion go free.

Gratitude is the sign of noble souls.

The Traveller and the Farmer

A traveller came upon a farmer hoeing in a field beside the road one afternoon. The traveller called out to say hello to the farmer, who looked up from his work. "How long will it take me to get to the next town?" asked the stranger.

"I can't really say," was the farmer's curt reply. Insulted, the traveller strode off.

"About an hour," shouted the farmer after him.

"Why didn't you say so when I first asked?"

"Because I didn't know how fast you were walking then."

The Fisherman and his Wife

Once upon a time, there was a poor fisherman who lived in a shack by the sea. One day, he caught a fish, which to his surprise spoke to him and begged to be allowed to return to the water.

The fisherman did as the fish asked, but when he told his wife, she was angry. "You should have asked for a wish!" she said. "I want to live in a castle. Go and wish for one."

The man went and called the fish and asked for his wish. And the fish said, "Go home. It is already done."

So the man went home and instead of the shack he found a stone castle. "Isn't it beautiful! Look at it all!" said his wife. And they enjoyed a feast and went to bed, happy with their grand new home.

The next morning the wife prodded her husband awake and said, "Get up. I want to be king! Go and ask the fish to grant me this wish." So the fisherman went and asked the fish, which said, "Go home. She is king already." When the fisherman came to where the castle had been he saw instead a gleaming palace. His wife was sitting on a huge silver throne, wearing a golden crown on her head.

The next morning, the fisherman's wife announced, "Husband, I know I am now the king but I want to be able to order the moon to rise and the sun to set – I want to be God."

Now the fisherman was afraid, but he had to go and ask the fish. The fish rose from the crashing waves and said, "What can your wife want now?"

"Alas," whispered the fisherman, quaking, "she wants to be God."

"Go," said the fish, "you will find her back again in the shack."

And there they are both living to this very day.

The Fox and the Stork

A fox and a stork were once good friends. One day, the fox invited the stork to dinner but to play a trick, he served soup in a shallow bowl. The fox could easily lap up his soup but the stork could do nothing with her long bill. She left the meal as hungry as when she arrived.

"I'm sorry," said the fox, laughing to himself, "that the soup is not to your liking."

"Do not apologize," said the stork, and they fixed a date when the fox would go for dinner at the stork's house.

When the day came, the stork served soup in a tall thin jug. The fox couldn't reach any of the delicious soup but the stork could easily fit her long, thin bill inside.

"I will not apologize," said the stork. "One bad turn deserves another."

Treat others as you would wish to be treated.

Nasreddin Hodja and the Pot

Nasreddin Hodja went to his neighbour to borrow a large cooking pot. When he returned it, the neighbour was surprised to find a smaller pot inside.

"What's this, Nasreddin?" he said.

"Oh, your pot gave birth while in my house," Nasreddin replied, "and naturally as the larger pot is yours, so the smaller pot belongs to you also."

'What a fool!' thought the man, but he smiled and accepted the pot.

Some days later, Nasreddin asked if he might borrow the pot again. After a few weeks, the neighbour went to ask for it back.

"Oh, I am sorry to tell you," said Nasreddin, "but your pot has died."

"Don't be so foolish" said the neighbour angrily. "Cooking pots don't die!"

"Are you sure?" said Nasreddin. "You didn't seem surprised when you heard it had given birth."

How the Town Became a Lake

Once upon a time, there was a town where there is now a lake. Its streets were full of beautiful houses and at the centre was a magnificent church. On Sundays, the golden bells in the church steeple and the songs of the choir rose to the mountains that surrounded the town.

But life was too easy for the people who lived there. They grew to care only for pleasure and forgot to look after the sick, the old and the feeble.

One day, a terrible thing happened. Water began to rise above the paving stones of the streets and to wash about the feet of the careless people. The water rose and rose until there was no town left! Instead there was a still lake, cradled by mountains. Sometimes, you can still hear bells ringing beneath the water.

A Silly Question

Dolly asked her little kitten, "How did you come to be white when all your brothers are tabby?"

"Well," the kitten began, "When we were very small we sought our fortune every night, and it turned out to be mice, mostly. One night I came to a hole I had never noticed before. I crept through it and found myself in a beautiful room. It smelled delicious. There was cheese there, and fish, and cream, and mice, and milk. It was the happiest hour of my life. But, as I was washing my face after a delicious herring's head, I noticed that on nails around the room were fur coats," the kitten said, trembling with fright.

Dolly stroked the kitten to make it speak faster.

"I stood there rooted to the ground with horror, and then came a sort of horrible barking and squeaking, and suddenly a terrible monster stood before me. It caught me up, and in less than a moment it had hung my tabby fur coat on a nail behind the door. I crept out of that lovely fairyland a cat without a fur coat. And that's how I came to be white."

"I don't quite see—" began Dolly.

"No? Why, what would your mother do if someone took off your coat, and hung it on a nail where she could not get it?"

"Buy me another, I suppose."

"Exactly. But when my mother took me to the cat fur coat shop, they were, unfortunately, out of tabby coats in my size, so I had to have a white one."

"I don't believe a word of it," said Dolly.

"What! You don't believe me? I'll never speak to you again," the kitten said. And it never has.

Simple Simon in London

Simple Simon had lived all his life in the country, but one day he decided to visit London. As he was walking around admiring the grand buildings, a maid opened one of the doors and a dog ran out of the house. It growled and snapped at Simple Simon, who bent down to pick up a stone to throw at the dog. But he found them all cemented in as cobblestones and could pry none of them loose.

"What a strange place London is," he said. "In the country we keep our dogs tied up and our stones loose, but here its the opposite — they keep their dogs loose and tie up their stones."

The Man and the Wooden God

Long, long ago, people used to worship statues. They would pray to them for luck and good fortune, and give offerings of food, wine and flowers.

There was a man who often prayed to a wooden statue that he had been given by his father. But no matter how hard he prayed, and no matter what offerings he left, his luck never changed.

One day, while the man was praying in front of the wooden god, he became frustrated and furious with its silence. In a temper, he went to the statue and with a single blow swept it down from its pedestal. The statue broke in two, and gold coins streamed from inside it.

"Ah!" the delighted man cried. "You do have some use after all!"

Usefulness is most men's test of worth.

The Gingerbread Man

One day, an old woman made a gingerbread man. She went to eat him once he had cooled but he hopped off the tray and ran out of the door! The old woman and her husband ran after him, but they couldn't catch him. "Run, run, as fast as you can! You can't catch me, I'm the gingerbread man!" it called. He ran and ran, and the old woman and her husband ran after him with their dog and cat, their cow, horse, pig and rooster. He kept on running until he came to the river. And then the gingerbread man had to stop.

"How can I cross the river?" The gingerbread man cried. A sly fox suddenly appeared by his side and said, "I could carry you across." So the gingerbread man jumped on the fox's nose and SNAP! the fox gobbled him up.

The Hut in the Forest

A woodcutter once lived with his wife and two daughters in a hut on the edge of a forest. Each morning the woodcutter would go out to work, and one of his daughters would bring him lunch. One day, however, his youngest daughter lost her way in the wood. She came to a little house and knocked on the door. A rough voice cried, "Come in."

When she opened the door, an old man was sitting at a table. Nearby were three animals – a hen, a cockerel, and a cow. The girl asked for shelter for the night and the old man said, "You can stay with us, share our supper and sleep here. But first, you have to cook our meal."

The girl prepared a supper – however, she didn't think of the animals. She carried two dishes to the

table, sat by the grey-haired man, and ate. When she finished, the man opened a trap-door and the girl landed in the cold cellar!

The next day, her worried sister came to find her. She too came across the hut in the wood, and the old man said the same thing to her. The sister prepared some soup for the grey-haired man and herself, but first she fed the cockerel, cow and hen. The old man thanked her and showed her to a room where she could spend the night.

In the morning there was a bright flash. The girl got up to see what had happened and met a handsome prince on the stairs. It was the old man, released from a spell. "A witch enchanted me and my servants." the prince said. "The spell could only be broken by a girl like you, whose heart is full of love for all living things. Now, I beg you to be my wife.

The girl was delighted, and so after her sister was brought up from the cellar they were married and lived happily ever after.

The Ugly Duckling

One day a batch of duck eggs hatched in a farmyard. Strangely, one chick was much bigger and uglier than the rest. The poor duckling was pecked and pushed about by all the other ducks — and the chickens too. "He's too big — and so ugly!" they clucked. The duckling was very sad, so he ran away.

He spent all winter alone, and slowly grew up but no one spoke to him. Then one day he looked down at his reflection in the water and saw he was no longer a grey, ugly duckling — he was a swan! He held his neck high and swam over to some other swans, who were calling to him. "I never dreamed I could be so happy when I was the ugly duckling!" he cried.

The Crow

Once there was a princess who loved to walk in the garden of a deserted castle. As she was strolling along one day, a black crow hopped out and said, "I am a prince under a witch's spell. Will you save me, Princess? You would have to say goodbye to all your own people and live in this ruined castle. You would be all by yourself, and if anything frightening happened you would not be able to scream or ask for help."

The good-natured princess felt she had to agree to try and help, so she hurried inside the ruined castle and waited for nightfall. At midnight a troop of goblins, sprites, imps, witches and trolls suddenly burst into the room she was resting in. They lit a fire and placed a cauldron of boiling water on it. Then they dragged the princess towards the cauldron. She nearly died with fright, but she never uttered a sound. Then all of a sudden the cockerel crowed, and the evil spirits vanished.

And so each day the princess sat alone in the castle, and at night bravely kept her silence. Then

one evening, she heard a rustling beside her — the crow had turned into a handsome youth.

"I am the prince," he said, "who you in your goodness, freed from the most awful torments. Stay with me here as my bride, and let us live happily together."

The princess said yes, and when she looked around her she couldn't believe she was in the same castle — for it had all been rebuilt and filled with beautiful furniture, cheerful servants and friends. And there they lived for many happy years.

A Day's Work

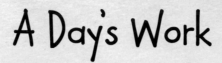

Aman once made a deal with a mean goblin that he hoped would make him very rich: if the man could find a job the goblin couldn't finish, the goblin would give him all his gold. If he failed, he would die. The goblin appeared at the man's house, and asked, "What's my work?"

The man threw ten thousand seeds over a nearby field, and said, "You must pick up every seed!"

This was an easy task for the goblin, and he soon returned to ask for a new task. The man took the goblin to a beach and told him to sweep up all the sand. The goblin did as he was asked and soon the man was in despair! His wife, however, said she had an idea, and she took one curly hair from her head, "Tell him to straighten this hair," she said.

All day long the goblin tried, but he couldn't do it – and the man was saved by his wife's cleverness.

The Two Neighbours

Long ago, two neighbours prayed to the great god Zeus. The god saw that one of the neighbours had a terrible greed for money and that the other neighbour was always envious. So, to teach them both a lesson, Zeus decided that he would grant each man whatever he wished, but the other neighbour would get twice as much.

The first, greedy neighbour wished for a room filled with gold and was amazed when it appeared before him! A few minutes later the second neighbour came to boast that two rooms of gold had appeared in his house. The second neighbour was instantly envious that the first neighbour had gold too, even though he had twice as much. So he wished that his neighbour might lose one eye. Of course, it was no sooner said than done – but he himself became totally blind.

Vices are their own punishment.

How the Hedgehog Beat the Hare

Ahedgehog once bet a hare that he could beat him in a race. The hare thought he could easily win, so he agreed. They met in a ditch, and the hedgehog explained they would run from one side to the other, until one of them gave up. The hare did not know that the hedgehog had asked his friend to wait on one side of the ditch, while he stood on the other. The race began, and when the hare reached the other side of the ditch, the hedgehog said, "Now back we go!" The crafty hedgehogs repeated this until the hare, puffing, announced, "You win!"

Anansi Finds some Meat

When Mother Hyena was away, Anansi, the trick-playing spider, went to the hyena's den and told the hyena's cubs he was their uncle, called You-all. "Wake me when your mother brings food," he said, and he went to sleep.

Mother Hyena soon came home with meat, which she gave to her cubs, saying, "This is for you all."

So the cubs woke Anansi and gave him the meat, which he gobbled up. Mother Hyena brought meat twice more, saying, "This is for you all." Each time, the cubs gave Anansi the meat.

In the evening when Mother Hyena came home, the cubs started crying for food.

"Still hungry after all the meat I gave you?" she asked, surprised.

"Uncle ate it all!" they wailed. 'Time to go!' thought Anansi and he sprinted away, very happy with his many meals.

Raggedy Ann and the Kittens

Raggedy Ann, the rag doll, and the other toys were sitting in the nursery when Fido the dog came in. "Guess what!" said Fido. "I went into the barn to hunt for mice, and found three tiny little kittens in an old basket in a dark corner!"

The toys could hardly wait until it was time for bed that night. Raggedy Ann suggested that all the dolls go down to the barn and see the kittens. This they did easily, for the window was open and it was only a short jump to the ground.

The dolls crawled through the hole in the barn door and ran to the basket. Just as Raggedy Ann reached down to pick up one of the kittens there was a lot of howling and yelping, and Fido came bounding through the hole with Mamma Cat hissing behind him.

"I'm surprised at you, Mamma Cat!" said Raggedy Ann, "Fido wouldn't hurt your kittens for anything!"

"I'm sorry, then," said Mamma Cat.

"Have you told the folks up at the house about your kittens?" Raggedy Ann asked.

"Oh, my, no!" exclaimed Mamma Cat.

"Let's take them into the house!" said Raggedy Ann, "and Mistress can find them there in the morning!"

"How lovely!" said all the dolls.

"Do take them to the house, Mamma Cat!"

So Raggedy Ann carried two of the kittens to the house while Mamma Cat carried the other. Fido insisted that Mamma Cat and the kittens should take over his nice, soft basket.

In the morning when Marcella, their mistress, came into the nursery, the first thing she saw were the three little kittens. She cried out in delight, and carried them off to show her Mamma and Daddy.

Mamma and Daddy said the kittens could stay in the nursery and belong to Marcella and she eventually decided upon three names – Prince Charming for the white kitty, Cinderella for the grey tabby and Princess Golden for the kitty with the yellow stripes. So that is how the three little kittens came to live in the nursery.

And Mamma Cat found out that Fido was a very good friend, too. She grew to trust him so much she would even let him help wash the kittens' faces.

The Fighting Birds and the Partridge

A man who kept poultry had two fighting cockerels among his birds. One day, by chance, he found a tame partridge for sale. He bought it and took it home to be reared with the cockerels. However, when the partridge was put into the poultry yard, the cockerels flew at it and followed it about, and the partridge became distressed.

Of course, the partridge thought that the cockerels were treating him so badly because he was a stranger. Yet, not long afterwards, he saw them fighting each other. They fought furiously, and did not quit until one had well and truly beaten the other. Then the partridge said to himself, "I won't get upset at being bullied by these birds, for they can't even stop quarrelling with each other."

Strangers should avoid those who quarrel among themselves.

King Thrushbeard

There was once a king who had a beautiful daughter. However, she thought that no one was good enough for her to marry. So one day, the king invited all the young men from near and far to see if they could find a match that she approved of — but the princess rejected them all. "He's too tall," she announced. "He's too short… He's too serious…" She even mocked a king with a very bushy beard, saying, "You should be called King Thrushbeard!"

Her father was angry that she was so rude, and said she must marry the next beggar that came to the palace.

A few days later a fiddler came to beg. The king made the princess marry him, and her new husband led her away down the road.

When they came to a huge forest, the fiddler said, "This forest belongs to King Thrushbeard."

Then they came to a large town, and the fiddler said, "This town belongs to King Thrushbeard."

The princess sighed, "If only I had chosen him!"

At last they came to a little hut, and the fiddler said, "This is your new home. You can start by making a fire and cooking the supper."

But the princess didn't know how to, so the fiddler had to help her. For a few days they muddled through, but then they ran out of money to buy food. "Go and work in the palace as a kitchen maid," the fiddler told her. "That way, we will get free food."

So the princess went to work in the royal kitchen, doing the dirtiest, most unpleasant jobs.

One day, the palace servants were told that the king was getting married. Candles were lit and guests in beautiful clothes arrived. The princess wished with all her heart that she had not been so horrible to everyone. After a busy morning in the kitchen, she went to the ballroom to see the grand wedding feast laid out on the tables.

Then the king, seeing her at the door, said, "It is me — the fiddler. I disguised myself in order to teach you a lesson."

Then the princess recognized him. She said, "I should never have been so proud and rude!"

The king took her hands in his and said, "Don't cry – it is all forgotten... and now it is time for us to get married properly."

Then maids-in-waiting helped the princess into a beautiful wedding dress, and her father and all his royal court arrived to celebrate the joyful day.

The Lad and the Devil

There was a lad who was walking along a road cracking nuts, when he met the Devil.

"Is it true," said the lad, "that you can climb into a nut hole?"

"Certainly," said the Devil.

"Then just creep into this nut," said the lad.

So the Devil did.

Now, when he had crept well in, the lad sealed up the nut with a pin.

Then the lad came to a blacksmith, and asked if he'd crack that nut for him.

"That I will," said the blacksmith, and he took his hammer and gave the nut a huge blow.

The nut flew into pieces with such a bang that half the roof blew off. "Why! I think the Devil was in that nut," said the blacksmith.

"He was, you're quite right," said the lad, and went away laughing.

The Drop of Water

Once there was an old man called Cribble-Crabble, who loved using his microscope to look at tiny things.

One day, he looked at a drop of muddy water through the microscope.

What a sight he saw! The water was actually filled with teeny-tiny creepy-crawly creatures. They wriggled and squirmed and crawled all over each other. It even looked as though some of them were fighting!

Cribble-Crabble called his next-door neighbour, who was a magician, to come in. He looked through the microscope and gasped.

"Oh my goodness!" he cried. "You've conjured up a tiny city full of strange angry creatures!"

"No!" cried Cribble-Crabble. "It's a drop of muddy water."

The magician couldn't decide whether the microscope was science or magic.

What do you think?

The Goose that Laid the Golden Eggs

Once upon a time, there lived a farmer who owned a prize goose. The goose laid an egg every day, and it was always big and tasty.

One morning, when the farmer went to check the nest, he was surprised to find that the egg was yellow and shiny. When he picked it up, it was as heavy as lead. He examined it closely, and to his surprise he saw that the egg was made of pure gold. To the farmer's amazement, the next day the goose laid another golden egg… and the next day… and the next… He soon became very wealthy from selling the eggs. However, as he grew richer, he became greedier. One day he decided he wanted to have all the gold the goose must have inside her at once – so he killed her only to find no gold at all.

Greedy people who try to take too much will often run out of luck.

Why the Swallow's Tail is Forked

The Great Spirit once asked all the animals that he had made to come to his lodge. "I often hear you complain," said the Great Spirit. "What do you wish me to do? How can I make things better?"

Man stepped forwards and said, "O Great Father, the serpent feasts upon my blood. Will you give him some other food instead?"

"The serpent must eat," said the Great Spirit. "Mosquito, you are a great traveller. Fly away and find out which creature's blood is best for the serpent."

The mosquito travelled over the earth and on his way bit every creature he could to find whose blood was the best. On his way back, he looked up and saw a swallow.

"I'm glad to see you, my friend," sang the swallow. "Have you found out whose blood is best for the serpent?"

"The blood of man," answered the mosquito.

The swallow had always been a friend of man, and he wanted to help him, so he tore out the mosquito's tongue!

When the Great Spirit asked the mosquito whose blood was best, the mosquito tried to say, 'The blood of man,' but he could not speak. He could only say, "Kss-ksss-ksssss!"

Then the swallow said, "Great Father, the mosquito is shy. I met him before we arrived here and he told me frog's blood is best for the serpent."

"The serpent shall have the frog's blood," said the Great Spirit. "Man shall no longer be his food."

The serpent was angry with the swallow — he didn't like frog's blood. So, as the swallow flew near him, he grabbed his tail and tore it! This is why the swallow's tail is forked, and why man always looks upon the swallow as a friend.

Sir Gammer Vans

Last Sunday morning at six o'clock in the evening as I was sailing over the mountains in my little boat, I visited Sir Gammer Vans. He lives in a brick house, built entirely of flint, standing alone by itself in the middle of sixty or seventy others. In the garden is an apple tree made of iron, covered in steel and pears.

"How d'ye do?" said he.

"Very well," said I.

"Have some breakfast?"

"With all my heart," said I.

So he gave me a slice of beer, and a cup of cold veal and showed me his little dog.

"He killed a hare today," he said, "And if you don't believe me, I'll show you the hare alive in a basket."

Then, we went shooting and I killed eighteen birds, besides a dead salmon that was flying over the bridge, out of which I made the best apple pie I ever tasted.

The Man
and the Eagle

An eagle was once captured by a man, who clipped his wings and put him in the poultry yard, along with the chickens. The eagle was very depressed about his change in fortune.

"Why should you be so sad?" said the man. "When you were an eagle, you were just ordinary but as an old rooster, you're the finest one I ever saw."

The Doll in the Grass

Once upon a time there was a king who had twelve sons. One day he told them they must all find themselves wives. There was one catch however — their wives must be able to spin, weave and make a shirt in one day, or else he would not accept them.

When the youngest son, Ashiepattle, went to seek a wife, he found a tiny doll in the grass sitting in a chair, looking very beautiful.

He told her his tale and said, "If you can make a shirt, will you become my wife?"

She said that she would, and set to work to get the shirt spun, woven and made. But when it was finished it was very, very tiny!

Ashiepattle returned home and showed it to the king. He was pleased with it, so Ashiepattle set out to fetch his bride. When he arrived to collect the doll he wanted her to sit with him on his horse, but she said she would travel in a silver spoon, drawn by two small white mice!

Ashiepattle was afraid he would ride over her — she was so very, very tiny.

When they had travelled a short way they came to a large lake. There, Ashiepattle's horse took fright and shied, knocking over the spoon. The poor little doll fell into the water! Ashiepattle was upset, for he did not know how to rescue her. He was just about to dive into the lake when a merman brought the her up to the water's surface. In front of Ashiepattie's eyes the little doll grew until she was normal-sized!

So Ashiepattle placed her in front of him on his horse and rode home. When they returned they were married, and they lived happily ever after.

The Thirsty Pigeon

There was once a pigeon who had flown for many miles without water. She was desperate for a drink, but could not find a lake, a pond or even a puddle to sip from. Suddenly, she noticed a goblet of water painted on a signboard. The pigeon had no idea that it was only a picture, so she flew towards it excitedly. *BANG!* She crashed right into the signboard, then slid to the ground, her head spinning. After that, the silly pigeon learnt to always take more care.

Enthusiasm should not outrun being cautious.

The Troll and the Bear

Once upon a time there was a troll who travelled to a farm in Norway every Christmas Eve. He would shove everyone out of the house, and sit by the fire eating frogs.

Then, one year, a man with a performing bear also arrived at the farm. The farmer told him about the troll but the man begged to be allowed to stay. Towards the evening, the troll came and sat down by the fire. The man pinched the bear's arm and the bear growled.

"Take care," said the man to the troll, "or he'll tear you into pieces."

The troll looked frightened and asked, "Are there more like him?"

"Yes," said the man, "but the others are much fiercer. They're on their way now."

The troll thought that he wouldn't much like to tackle more than one bear, so he left in a hurry and has never shown himself since.

The Dog and his Reflection

Once upon a time a dog found a piece of meat and decided to carry it home in his mouth to eat in peace. After a while he came across a stream and trotted along beside it.

As the dog walked along he looked down at the water, then stopped in surprise. There was another dog with a piece of meat looking up at him from the water! The dog had no idea it was his own reflection. His only thought was that he had to have the other piece of meat too. He made a snap at the dog in the water, but as he opened his mouth he dropped the meat. It plopped into the stream and sank!

It is very foolish to be greedy.

JULY

Lazy Jack

There was once a boy who was known as Lazy Jack. He never did any work, until one day his mother told him to go and work for the neighbouring farmer. At the end of the day the farmer paid him with a wheel of cheese. Jack carried it home in his hat, which he put on his head. By the time he got home it had melted.

"You should have held it in your hands," said his mother, shaking her head.

The next day the farmer paid Jack with a cat. Jack carried the cat home in his hands but it scratched until he let go, so he lost it. When he got home, his mother said, "You should have walked it home on a string."

"I'll do so another time," said Jack.

The next day, the farmer gave Jack a leg of lamb as payment. Jack tied it to a string, and trailed it along after him in the dirt, so that by the time he got home it was completely spoilt.

"You silly boy!" said his mother,"You should have carried it on your shoulder."

"I'll do so another time," replied Jack.

The day after the farmer gave Jack a donkey. So with some trouble Jack hoisted the donkey onto his shoulder and started walking home.

Now, it just so happened Jack passed a house where a rich man lived with his daughter, who could not hear or speak. The doctors said she would be cured if she could be made to laugh. The girl saw Jack passing by, with the donkey on his shoulders, kicking and hee-hawing and she burst into great fits of laughter. Immediately she recovered her speech and hearing! Her father was overjoyed, and let her marry Lazy Jack, who was made a rich gentleman. They lived in a large house, and Jack's mother lived with them in great happiness.

The Khoja's Robe

One day the Khoja's wife washed his robe and hung it on a tree branch to dry in the garden of the house. That night when the Khoja went out, he thought he saw a robber climbing down the tree. He shouted to his wife, "Quick, give me my bow and arrows!"

Then he went outside and shot at the robe, piercing it through and through. The Khoja returned to the house, happy he had dealt with the burglar. The next morning, he discovered that it was his own robe he had shot at, and exclaimed, "What a narrow escape! If I had been wearing my robe, I would have shot myself!"

The Crow and the Serpent

A very hungry crow used up what little energy he had left to find food. Imagine how relieved he was when he noticed a serpent asleep in a sunny nook. Swooping down, the crow seized it greedily.

The serpent was not about to die without a fight, however, and it suddenly darted forward, biting the crow and delivering a mortal wound.

The crow died in agony from the venom saying, "Oh, unhappy me! I thought I had got lucky but in fact I had brought about my own downfall!"

What seems to be a blessing is not always the case.

The Problem of the Gordian Knot

The people of Phrygia had a great wonder — an ox-cart tied to a pole with a wonderfully intricate knot of dried bark. It had been said that anyone who could untie the knot would become king of all Asia. But how could anyone undo it when the bark was too brittle to be moved, and the ends were tucked somewhere in the middle of the knot?

Many men considered the problem but no one could do it. Then the greatest warrior of the ancient world, Alexander, came riding into town with his army. He was told the story, and demanded to be taken to the knot. "This is how I solve the puzzle!" he declared, and taking his sword he sliced the knot in two. Ever since, cutting the Gordian knot means finding a simple solution to an impossible problem.

Tom Thumb

A poor woodcutter and his wife had a teeny-tiny baby boy, who grew up to be no bigger than a thumb, so they called Tom Thumb. Small as he was, the couple loved him dearly. Tom was good and thoughtful, and helped his parents as best he could.

One day, he went to help his father cart logs. He sat by the horse's ear shouting, "Gee up!" to drive the horse home. But two men, who were passing, saw Tom and thought they could show him at fairs for money and make their fortune.

When the woodcutter wasn't looking, they carried Tom off but the first time they sat down to rest, Tom snuck out of the man's pocket and hid in a snail shell until they'd gone. Then he started to walk the long, long way home.

Before long a wolf crept up on him and threatened to eat him up in one big gulp. Tom thought hard, and quickly came up with a plan. "My friend," he called out, as loud as he could. "I know where more tasty treats are to be found."

"Tell me more, whoever you are," replied the wolf.

So Tom described his parents' cottage and where it was. "When you find it, you can crawl through the drain into the kitchen, and then into the pantry," he suggested. "There you will find ham, beef, cold chicken, roast pig, cakes, apple cider, and everything that your heart can wish for."

So the wolf sped away to the woodcutter's cottage, with Tom Thumb on his back. The wolf crawled through the drain into the kitchen and into the pantry. There he ate and drank to his heart's content. But when he tried to squeeze back out through the drain, he found that his stomach was now so big and full that he would not fit, no matter how hard he tried.

That was just what Tom had counted on, and now he began to shout at the top of his voice:

"Father! Mother! It's me, Tom! I'm in the pantry with a wolf."

The woodcutter and his wife awoke at once and went down to the kitchen. The woodcutter thanked the wolf for returning Tom and in a flash of his axe the wolf was dead.

The Fox and the Grapes

A **fox was strolling** through an orchard when he noticed a bunch of juicy grapes. The fox licked his lips. "Those delicious grapes would be just the thing to quench my thirst," he said to himself. But the only problem was, he couldn't reach them.

Nevertheless, the fox was determined to have the grapes for himself. He jumped as high as he could, but just missed.

Again and again he jumped and tried to reach the grapes, until he was quite worn out. All the creatures in the orchard were laughing.

At last, the fox had to admit defeat and gave up. As he walked away to the sound of sniggering, he stuck his nose in the air and said, "I am sure those grapes are sour, anyway."

It is easy to look down on what you cannot get.

The Sheep and the Pig

Once there was a big sheep who lived on a farm, and one morning the farmer said to his wife, "Let's eat that sheep tomorrow."

The big sheep heard these words, and was scared, so he went and told the pig the news.

"Let's run away to the woods," the pig said. "I can chop trees and we can build a house together."

So off they went. When they had gone a little way, a hare ran up to them.

"Good-day," said the sheep. "We're going to build a house in the woods."

"I'll go with you," said the hare, "I have teeth to gnaw pegs, and paws to hammer them. I'll be the carpenter."

So they set off to the woods to build the house. The pig cut the logs, the sheep pulled them home and the hare put them together.

And they all lived happily together because there is no place like home.

The Bat and the Weasels

One evening, a bat flew straight into a tree and fell to the ground. Before the bat could fly away again, a weasel caught him.

The bat begged to be released but the weasel said he couldn't do that because he was an enemy of the birds. "I'm not a bird, I'm a mouse," said the bat.

The weasel looked at the bat. "So you are," he said, and he let the bat go.

Soon after, the bat was caught in the same way by another weasel, and begged for his life.

"No," said the weasel, "I never let a mouse go."

"I'm not a mouse," said the bat, "I'm a bird."

The weasel examined the bat. "So you are," he said, and he too let the bat go.

It is often wise to use your circumstances to your advantage.

The All Dog

A lion once saw a poodle and, very rudely, burst into laughter at how ridiculous he looked.

"Whoever saw so small a beast?" said the lion.

"It is very true," said the poodle, with dignity, "that I am small; but, sir, I have to point out that you are only a largish type of cat. I am all dog."

The Two Frogs

In Japan there lived two frogs, one in the town of Osaka, the other in Kyoto. One day, both frogs decided they wanted to visit the other town. Halfway there they had to climb a high mountain. At the top, they bumped into each other and started talking.

They both wished to know if the town was worth visiting. "If we stand up and hold on to each other, maybe we can see them," suggested one frog, so they did that.

Each frog could now see a town, but what they didn't realize was that although their noses pointed towards the town they were travelling to, their eyes were looking back at their own.

Each frog thought that the town they were looking at looked exactly like their own (because it was) and so they gave up their journeys.

Tikki Tikki Tembo

In China there lived two brothers, one named Sam, and one named Tikki Tikki Tembo No Sarimbo Hari Kari Bushkie Perry Pem Do Hai Kai Pom Pom Nikki No Meeno Dom Barako.

The two brothers were once playing near a well and Tikki Tikki Tembo No Sarimbo Hari Kari Bushkie Perry Pem Do Hai Kai Pom Pom Nikki No Meeno Dom Barako fell in. Sam shouted, "Quick, Tikki Tikki Tembo No Sarimbo Hari Kari Bushkie Perry Pem Do Hai Kai Pom Pom Nikki No Meeno Dom Barako has fallen into the well! Help!"

The gardener grabbed a ladder and climbed into the well to rescue him. He pulled Tikki Tikki Tembo No Sarimbo Hari Kari Bushkie Perry Pem Do Hai Kai Pom Pom Nikki No Meeno Dom Barako out — but he had nearly drowned! Ever since then, the Chinese have given their children short names.

Finding Raggedy Andy

One day, Daddy took Raggedy Ann down to his office and propped her up against some books on his desk. He wanted to have her where he could see her cheery smile all day.

Just as Daddy was finishing his day's work, a package arrived. Daddy opened it and found a letter from Grandma, which said that at the time Raggedy Ann was made, a neighbour had made a boy doll called Raggedy Andy, which she enclosed.

His soft, floppy arms were folded up in front of him, and his legs were folded over his arms. They were held this way by a rubber band.

After slipping off the rubber band, Daddy smoothed out the wrinkles in Raggedy Andy's arms and legs. Then he propped Raggedy Ann and Raggedy Andy up against books on his desk, so they sat facing each other — Raggedy Ann's shoe button eyes looking straight into the shoe button eyes of Raggedy Andy.

They could not speak to each other in front of Daddy – so they just sat there and smiled at each other. "So, Raggedy Ann and Raggedy Andy," said Daddy, "I will go away and let you get reacquainted."

Daddy then took the rubber band and placed it around Raggedy Ann's right hand, and around Raggedy Andy's right hand.

Daddy knew they would like to tell each other all the wonderful things that had happened since they had parted more than fifty years ago, so he left the two rag dolls looking into each other's eyes. The next morning, when Daddy unlocked his door, he saw that Raggedy Andy had fallen over so that he lay with his head cuddled into the bend of Raggedy Ann's arm.

The Man and his Wives

Long, long ago, it was the custom for a man to have many wives. In these times, there was a middle-aged man who had two wives – one old and one young.

Now there came a time when the man's hair began to turn grey. The young wife did not like this at all as she thought it made him look too old. Every night she combed his hair and picked out all the grey ones.

However, the older wife was pleased that her husband was going grey. This was because people had sometimes mistaken her for his mother! Every morning, she combed the man's hair and picked out the brown ones.

Of course, there was only one result – the man soon ended up entirely bald!

Give what you have to all and you will soon have nothing to give.

The Jumpers

Once upon a time, a flea, a grasshopper and a goose decided to hold a jumping competition against each other. The king said he would give his daughter's hand in marriage to the creature who jumped the highest.

The flea jumped first — and he went so high that nobody could see him. The grasshopper only jumped half as high as the flea.

The goose stood still for a long time then all of a sudden the court dog gave him a nudge and — *PLOP!* he jumped sideways, straight into the lap of the princess.

"Splendid!" cried the king. "To jump up to my daughter is the highest jump that can be made. It takes brains to get an idea like that — and the goose has shown that he does have brains."

So the jumping goose won the princess.

Little Topknot

Once a cockerel and some hens lived in a farmyard. One hen had a pretty topknot that she was very proud of, so she strutted about a lot.

One day she said, "I'm tired of this farmyard. I want the world to see me. I shall fly over the fence."

The cockerel said, "Don't go!"

All the old hens said, "Don't go-go-go!"

But little Topknot flew over the fence and carried on strutting down the road.

Just then a hawk flew over her head. He saw little Topknot all alone, so he flew down and caught her in his claws! The farmer came running and frightened the hawk away, but the hawk had scratched her pretty topknot with his claws.

Little Topknot was very glad to get back to the farmyard. Now she doesn't strut about, but scratches for seeds instead.

The Fisherman
and the Bottle

A poor fisherman out in his boat one morning, caught nothing but a strange brass bottle, sealed with a cork. Curiously, he tugged at the cork and opened the bottle. At that moment, smoke came out of the bottle, and quickly formed itself into the shape of a huge genie.

"At last I am free!" it roared, "Now I will kill you!"

The fisherman thought quickly. "That's a fancy trick, the way you came out of that bottle," he said. "I bet you couldn't ever get back into it."

"Of course I could," said the Genie.

"Prove it," said the fisherman and the Genie coiled himself back into the small bottle.

Quickly the fisherman rammed the cork in, and threw the bottle back into the sea.

Jupiter and the Tortoise

Long ago, when the great god Jupiter ruled the Earth, the time came when he was to marry. Jupiter invited all the animals to the wedding. The day arrived, the ceremony was performed, and then everyone gathered for the banquet. Jupiter noticed that one animal was missing — the tortoise. The feast was a success, but Jupiter was sad that the tortoise had not turned up, so he went to ask him why.

"I don't care for going out," said the tortoise, "there's no place like home."

Jupiter was enraged by this reply, and declared that from then on the tortoise should carry his house on his back, and never be able to get away from his home even if he wished to.

Be careful what you say, people might take you at your word.

The Darning Needle

Once, there lived a darning needle who saw itself as something quite special.

One day the cook used the needle to mend an old slipper and its tip broke off, so the cook pinned her shawl together with it.

"Now I'm a brooch!" said the needle. "I knew I was important!"

But the very next day it dropped off the cook's shawl in the street and lay in the gutter. Soon, however, a boy picked the needle up and stuck her in a eggshell to make a boat and mast. "Wonderful! People can see how important I am," it cried.

But at that very moment – CRACK! a bicycle ran over the eggshell. The darning needle was shattered into tiny pieces, and no one got to see it after all!

The Top and the Ball

A spinning top and a ball lay together in a box. "Shall we be married, as we live together?" said the top. But the ball thought a lot of herself and would not even reply.

The next day, a little boy came along. He painted the top red and yellow so that while it was spinning around it looked quite splendid.

The day after, the ball was taken out by the boy. The top watched the ball bouncing high in the air, like a bird but then the boy lost it on a great big bounce. He searched everywhere for the ball, but it could not be found – it was gone.

Several years passed by, and the top was no longer young – so the boy painted him a beautiful gold colour. From time to time the spinning top thought of the ball that he once loved.

But then one day the top spun out of control, and then he, also, was gone. The top had fallen into a dustbin, where all sorts of rubbish lay about along with dust, leaves and other things, which had fallen down from the gutter under the roof.

"Now I am in a fix," he said. And then he glanced at a curious round thing, like an old apple, which lay nearby. It was, however, not an apple, but the old ball, which had lain for years in the gutter and now was soaked through with water. Looking at it, the top realized he no longer loved the proud ball.

A woman then came to clean out the dustbin. "Ah," she exclaimed, "here is the spinning top." So the top was taken back into the house, but nothing more was heard of the ball.

Hercules and the Waggoner

A waggoner was carefully driving along his heavy cart when the wheels sank in the mud. He set his shoulder to the cart and urged the horse forwards, but the wheels sank deeper.

The waggoner prayed to the ancient hero Hercules, who was famous for his great strength.

"Hercules, please help me!" he cried.

"You called?" came a booming voice.

The waggoner spun around to see a giant of a man, with a lion skin wrapped round his shoulders. Hercules – for it was he – said, "Don't just stand there. I'm not going to do it for you! Set your shoulder to the wheel for one more push, and this time I'll help."

Fate helps those who help themselves.

The Turtle's Rescue

There were once four animals that were great
friends — a deer, a crow, a turtle, and a mouse.
One day, a hunter captured the turtle, tied him up
then set off towards home.

The three remaining friends quickly worked out a
scheme to set the turtle free. The deer laid himself in
the road, pretending to be dead with the crow
pecking at his head. The mouse waited nearby to
bite through the rope that was holding the
turtle. The hunter saw the deer as he travelled
along the road, and setting down the
turtle, he walked toward the deer to
collect it. As the
hunter got near,
the crow flew away, and the deer
ran off. Cursing his bad luck, the
hunter went back to get the turtle,
but the mouse had
chewed through the ropes! The man
found that the turtle had
disappeared. And so the four
friends were reunited.

The Miller with the Golden Thumb

An unkind merchant was sitting in an inn with a miller. He turned, and said to his companion, "Sir, I have heard that every honest miller has a golden thumb."

The miller said that was true.

Then the merchant said, "Then please, let me see your thumb." And when the miller showed it to him, the merchant said, "I can't see that your thumb is gold. It is the same as other men's thumbs!"

The miller answered, "The truth is that my thumb is gold, but you will not be able to see it, for it looks like an ordinary thumb to a fool."

Well, that silenced the merchant!

The Boy and the Fox

A boy saw a fox asleep on a hillside. He looked at it for a little while, thinking, then picked up a stone and said out loud, "I'll kill this fox, then I'll sell its fur to get some money. I'll buy seed with the money, and I'll sow them in my father's field. The people who pass by will see my wheat and they'll say, 'What fine wheat that boy has'. Then I'll say to them, 'Keep out of my wheat field.' But maybe they will not obey, so then I'll shout, 'Keep out of my wheat field!'

But the boy shouted this last part so loudly that the fox woke with a start. It ran away to the woods before the boy could grasp one of its hairs.

The Glass Coffin

There was once a young man who decided to go off travelling, but he soon became lost in a great forest. He was just starting to worry when a stag bounded up to him, swept him up on his great antlers, and carried him away to a huge mountain cave. The cave contained many bottles filled with blue gas, and in the middle stood two glass chests.

In the first chest was a model of a tiny castle, surrounded by a miniature village. Inside the second chest lay a beautiful young woman! Suddenly she opened her eyes. "Oh, thank goodness!" she cried. "Please help me out of this prison."

The man hurried to release her.

"I am the daughter of a rich nobleman," she explained. "One evening a stranger came and asked to marry me. I refused him and he cast a spell to trap me in this glass coffin. Then he changed my brother into a stag and shrunk my castle and village, putting them into the other glass chest. After, he turned all my people into smoke and trapped them in bottles. I fell into a deep, enchanted sleep but at last, you have set me free! Please help me carry the glass chest with my castle outside."

The young man helped the girl. Once they were outside, they watched the castle, houses, and farms quickly grow.

The young woman opened the glass bottles and the blue smoke rushed out and changed into people. As they hugged each other, a handsome young man came striding out of the forest. It was the girl's brother! He explained how he had fought and killed the evil magician at last.

And on that very day, the beautiful noblewoman married the young man who had saved her, and they lived happily ever after, with her brother, in the castle.

The Horse and his Rider

A young man fancied himself as a good rider so one market day he looked for a horse to buy. He found one he liked and was determined to ride it.

The young man did not know that the horse had not been properly broken in, however, and he didn't think to ask. He just climbed a nearby fence and dropped onto the horse's back.

The second the horse felt the rider's weight in the saddle, it set off at full gallop. One of the rider's friends saw him thundering down the road. Surprised, he called out, "Where are you off to in such a hurry?"

Gasping for breath, the young man pointed to the stallion, and replied, "I have no idea – you will have to ask the horse."

Act in haste and you will have to go with the consequences.

The Swineherd

A prince yearned to marry the daughter of the emperor. He sent her two presents – a perfect single rose and a bird, which had the sweetest song in the world. Foolishly, the spoilt princess was disappointed because neither present was made of gold or diamonds.

When the prince heard the news, he wasn't put off. He found himself a position as the emperor's swineherd, and while he watched the pigs he made a metal cooking pot with bells all around it. When the pot boiled, the bells played a tune, and you could smell the food being cooked in every home in the city.

The princess heard the bells and sent a lady-in-waiting down to the people to find out where the sound was coming from. When the maid returned and told the princess about the swineherd's magic pot, the princess declared she must have it at once. But then the lady-in-waiting said, "The swineherd said the pot's price is ten kisses, which must come from you."

So the princess gave the swineherd ten kisses and he gave her the pot.

A few days later, the princess heard music floating up to her window again. This time the swineherd had made a magic rattle – whenever anyone shook it, they could play any piece of music ever composed. This time the swineherd wanted a hundred kisses for it.

So the princess went to the pigsties. The ladies-in-waiting stood around the couple, and held out their skirts so that the princess and swineherd were hidden as they kissed. However, the emperor stood on his balcony just at that moment, and saw what was going on. He was furious, and threw both the swineherd and his daughter out of the palace! The couple stood outside the gates and the princess sobbed, "Oh why was I so foolish? I wish I had married the prince who sent me the gifts after all!"

The swineherd washed his face and pulled his prince's garments on. Then he went to comfort the princess.

He was now so handsome, she couldn't take her eyes off him! "I am the prince who sent you the rose and the bird," he explained. "Now you have learnt your lesson, I forgive you for being so silly." And he took the princess back to his kingdom and married her, and they lived happily ever after.

Sleeping Beauty

Long ago, a king and queen held a grand christening for their new baby daughter. They invited twelve fairies, but left out the thirteenth, who was known for being very mean.

One by one each fairy gave the baby a gift, such as goodness, beauty and intelligence. The twelfth fairy was about to step forwards, when suddenly, in strode the thirteenth fairy. She cried out, "When the princess is sixteen she shall prick her finger on a spindle and fall down dead." Then she disappeared in a flash!

The twelfth fairy spoke up quickly. "Perhaps I can soften this evil spell a little…" And her wish was that the princess would not die if she was to touch a spindle. Instead, she would fall asleep for a hundred years.

Well, the little princess grew up good and clever and beautiful — and everyone loved her. But on her sixteenth birthday, she came across a little door. Inside sat an old lady, busy at a strange wheel with some thread.

"What is this?" said the princess, reaching out for the spindle. "Ouch!" she cried as it pricked her finger.

Straightaway she fell into an enchanted sleep, as did everyone else in the palace. Years went by – and people often told stories of the beautiful sleeping Briar Rose (so the king's daughter was called).

On the very day that one hundred years had passed, a prince rode past. He cut his way through the bushes, which surrounded the palace, and walked through the still courtyard and the motionless halls. Finally, he came to the room where Princess Briar Rose lay asleep. The prince gently kissed her and at that moment she opened her eyes. Together they went out into the palace – everyone else was waking up too! Soon, a splendid feast was held to celebrate Briar Rose's marriage to the prince, and everyone lived happily ever after.

The Two Fellows and the Bear

Once upon a time, two men were travelling through a wood together when all at once, a huge bear rushed out at them.

One man ran for his life, but the other man threw himself to the ground, face down in the dust.

He kept very still, not even daring to breathe. The bear came up to him, sniffing him all over but at last it slouched off. It thought the man was dead, and bears do not like dead meat. Then, when the man who had run away saw that the bear had left, he came back laughing. "What was it the bear whispered to you?" he asked.

"It told me," said the other man, "a friend who runs off and leaves you at the first sign of trouble should not be trusted."

Never trust a friend who deserts you at a pinch.

The Soldier and his Horse

It was wartime, and a soldier looked after his horse with great care. He gave it oats, and exercised it every single day, for he wished the horse to be strong.

However, when the war was over, the soldier made the horse work hard. He gave it only chaff to eat and hardly ever brushed its coat.

The time came when war broke out again. The soldier saddled his horse for battle. He loaded it with his pack and weapons, but the half-starved beast sank under the soldier's weight.

"You will have to go to battle on foot," said the horse. "Due to hard work and bad food, you have turned me into a donkey, and you cannot in a moment turn me into a horse again."

When you have something that is of value, always look after it properly.

The Glow Worm and the Jackdaw

A jackdaw swooped down on a glow worm and was about to eat him.

"Wait a moment," said the glow worm, "and I'll tell you something."

"What is it?" said the jackdaw with interest.

"There are many glow worms in this forest. If you want lots to eat, follow me."

"Certainly!" said the jackdaw.

Then the glow worm led him to a place in the wood where a fire had been lit, and pointing to the sparks flying about, said, "Look, you can see the glow worms warming themselves. Help yourself."

The jackdaw darted at the sparks and tried to swallow them, but his mouth was so badly burned that he flew away saying, "Ah, the glow worm is a dangerous little creature!"

AuGuST

The Mountains in Turmoil

Once upon a time, a group of villagers built their homes around the base of some towering mountains. The mountains were like giants – huge and threatening – but the villagers didn't want to move anywhere else because the earth around the mountains was rich, and crops grew well.

One day, smoke started to pour from the mountain tops, the earth began to quake and rocks came tumbling down. The people were terrified that the mountains had come to life. Suddenly the earth shook violently and a huge gap appeared in the side of the mountains. The people fell to their knees and waited for the end to come.

At long last, a teeny tiny mouse poked its head and whiskers out of the gap and came scampering towards them.

And that was the end of it!

There is often much fuss about nothing.

The Key to the Storehouse

A rich farmer's son was looking for a wife. He had taken a liking to a local girl and went to visit her family. As he sat in their home, he saw lots of flax waiting to be spun. "How long does it take your daughter to spin that much flax?" he said.

"Oh, she'll do it in a day," said the mother proudly. The boy was surprised, and when he left, he slipped an old key he found on the floor into the bundle the flax.

Six weeks later he came back for another visit. The mother said, "You know, after your last visit the key to our storehouse went missing. We've looked everywhere. Then boy went over to the bundle of flax and pulled out the key.

"Obviously here a day lasts six weeks," he said. Do you think he married the girl after?

Little Red Riding Hood

Once upon a time there was a little girl who always wore a red riding cloak with a hood, so everyone called her Little Red Riding Hood.

One day, the girl's mother asked her to take a basket of food to her grandmother, who was poorly. Little Red Riding Hood set off through the woods to her house.

She hadn't gone very far, however, when she met a wolf. "Hello, little girl," the wolf said, licking his lips, "Where are you going?"

"To my grandmother's," Little Red Riding Hood replied. That gave the wolf an idea. He wanted to catch them both, so he ran ahead and when he reached the grandmother's house, he knocked on the door.

As soon as the door was open, the wolf gobbled her up whole, pulled on her clothes and climbed into her bed!

Little Red Riding Hood arrived at the cottage soon after, and found her grandmother with her nightcap pulled low and the covers drawn up over her chin, looking very odd.

"Grandmother," Little Red Riding Hood said, "what big ears you have!"

"All the better to hear you with," came the reply.

"Grandmother, what big eyes you have!"

"All the better to see you with," came the reply.

"Grandmother, what a big mouth you have!"

"All the better to eat you with!" roared the wolf. And he sprang out of bed and swallowed Little Red Riding Hood whole. Luckily, a huntsman was passing the cottage. He saw the wolf, took out his axe and killed it. Then – *slash* – he cut open the wolf's stomach and out tumbled Little Red Riding Hood and her grandmother, both safe and well!

The Gnat and the Lion

A brave little gnat flew up to a lion and said, "I am not afraid of you. I'm stronger than you. If you don't believe it, let us fight and see." With that, the gnat darted in and bit the lion's nose.

When the lion felt the sting, he was furious.

However, in his haste to swat the gnat, he only succeeded in scratching his nose and making it bleed. He failed altogether to hurt the gnat, which buzzed off in triumph.

The gnat's celebrations were short-lived, however. It flew straight into a spider's web, and was caught and eaten by the spider. And so the gnat was caught by an insignificant creature after having triumphed over the King of the Beasts.

No one is so great that they cannot fail.

Raiko Slays the Demon

In the country of Japan there lived a brave young warrior and clever archer called Raiko. He became a palace guard at a time when the emperor was troubled by a fearsome monster.

This dreadful beast had the wings of a bird, the body of a tiger, a monkey's head, a serpent's tail, and dragon's scales. None of the guards dared to face it but the young archer decided to fight the beast. He strung his bow and stood guard alone.

Towards midnight, the sharp eye of the archer saw the beast on the roof. He shot an arrow at it, and it fell. Then he rushed up and killed it.

Raiko was promoted to captain of the guard, and given a gold sword. To this day the children in Japan tell many tales of his skill and bravery.

The Farmer and the Money-lender

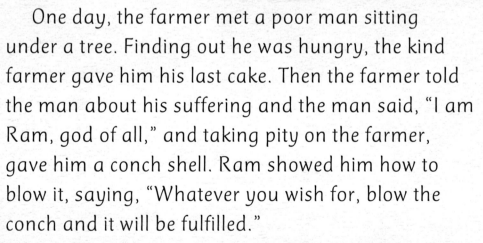

There was once a farmer who suffered at the hands of a money-lender. Good harvests or bad, the farmer was always poor, and the money-lender was always rich.

One day, the farmer met a poor man sitting under a tree. Finding out he was hungry, the kind farmer gave him his last cake. Then the farmer told the man about his suffering and the man said, "I am Ram, god of all," and taking pity on the farmer, gave him a conch shell. Ram showed him how to blow it, saying, "Whatever you wish for, blow the conch and it will be fulfilled."

The farmer went back to his village rejoicing.

The money-lender, however, noticed his high spirits at once, and worked away until he learnt the secret of the conch shell. Then he hatched a plan. He stole the conch, and said to the farmer, "I've got

your shell, but I can't use it. I promise to give you back your conch on one condition — whatever you get from it, I am to get double."

At last, the farmer was forced to give in. From that time, no matter what he gained, the money-lender gained double. At last there came a very dry season. The farmer blew his conch and wished for a well. And lo! one appeared, but the money-lender had two beautiful new wells!

This was too much for any farmer to stand, and he brooded over it till at last a bright idea came into his head. The farmer blew the conch, and cried out, "Oh, Ram! I wish to be blind in one eye!" And so he was — but the money-lender, of course, was blind in both, and in trying to steer his way between his two new wells, he fell into one, and drowned.

New Shoes

A man needed some new shoes, so he headed to the market place to buy a pair. Before he went, he drew a picture of his feet on a piece of paper, and added his measurements. Then, he set off on foot for the market. When he got there, he unhappily discovered that he had forgotten to bring piece of paper! He turned around and walked back many miles to get it. By the time he returned, the stalls were all packing up. He explained his situation to one of the stallkeepers. "But how did you get to market?" asked the stallkeeper.

"I walked," said the man.

"Then you brought your feet with you," said the stallkeeper. "Why did you need the paper?"

The man blushed, "I suppose I trusted my measurements more than the real thing."

The Goatherd
and the Goat

One day, a goatherd was out
on a mountainside where
his goats had been grazing.
It was time to round them
up and take them down to
the lowlands for the night.

However, one of the goats had
strayed off and was refusing to join the rest.

The goatherd tried to get her back by calling,
but the goat took no notice of him. He grew more
and more annoyed, until at last he lost his temper,
picked up a stone and threw it at her. To his horror,
he saw that he had broken one of her horns.

The goatherd begged the goat not to tell his
master, but she replied, "You silly boy, my broken
horn will tell what's happened, even if I keep quiet."

It's no use trying to hide
what can't be hidden.

The Clever Monkey and the Boar

Long, long ago in Japan, there lived a travelling man, who earned his living by taking round a monkey and showing off the animal's tricks. One evening the man came home in a bad temper, saying he was fed up with the monkey and would send for the butcher in the morning.

Now, the monkey was in the next room and overheard every word of the conversation. He said to himself, "I must go and talk to the wise boar in the forest about what to do."

The monkey slipped out of the house and spoke to the boar, who thought for a while and said, "I have it! I will creep into the house and steal their precious baby, and then you can rescue it from me."

The next morning

everything happened as planned. The husband and wife saw the boar steal their baby, then they saw the monkey running after the thief as hard as his legs would carry him.

Their gratitude knew no bounds when the faithful monkey brought the child safely back to their arms.

"There!" said the wife. "This is the animal you wanted to get rid of – if the monkey hadn't been here we would have lost our child forever."

"You are right, wife. He will be our honoured guest from now on," said the man, as he carried the child into the house.

The monkey was petted and lived the rest of his days in peace, and his master never did complain about him again.

The Lion and the Goat

A lion was attacking and eating all of the animals in a country so an old goat came up with a plan to stop it. "Please do it!" all the animals said.

The old goat lay down in a cave, and when the lion saw him, he stopped in his tracks. "So you have come," said the goat. "What do you mean?" said the lion.

"I have eaten one hundred elephants, one hundred tigers and ninety-nine lions so far. I have been waiting for one more lion —you!" said the goat, and he moved as if he were about to spring up.

The lion jumped back, thinking, 'It looks like an old goat, but it must be a wicked spirit to have eaten all those animals.'

Then the goat said, "Come here!"

"No way," said the lion, and he ran away!

The Astronomer

There was once an astronomer who enjoyed going out to watch the stars. He liked to walk in the countryside where there was no light at all, then he would make himself comfortable and spend hours watching the heavens.

One night, the astronomer was walking along gazing at the sky as usual. He was so absorbed with looking up that he fell into a dry well.

He lay there groaning until luckily a traveller passed by. The traveller looked down, and asked the astronomer what had happened.

But when the astronomer explained, the traveller said, "If you were looking so hard at the sky that you didn't even see where your feet were taking you, it appears to me that you deserve all you've got."

We should never aim so high that we miss the things around us.

Tinsel and Lightning

A piece of tinsel on a rock once said to a pebble, "You see how glittery bright I am! By birth I am related to the lightning."

"Indeed!" said the pebble, "How special you must be."

Sometime after, a flash of lightning struck the rock, and the tinsel was scorched by the flash and lost all its brilliancy.

"Where is your brilliant glitter now?" said the pebble.

"Oh, it is gone to the skies," said the tinsel, "I have lent it to the lightning that came down a moment ago to borrow it from me."

Soup from a Sausage Skewer

Long ago there was a lady-mouse, who stood talking to another lady-mouse, about a splendid feast that had just taken place in the mouse-king's palace. "It was wonderful!" she said to her friend. "We had fantastic food. There was stale bread for starters and wax candle for the main course. Pudding was mouldy sausages. In the end there was nothing left except the skewers that the sausages had been stuck on for grilling!"

The lady mouse continued, "After dinner everyone started talking about an old recipe — soup made from sausage skewers. Then the mouse-king stood on an old reel of thread and said that the lady-mouse who could make the tastiest soup from a sausage skewer would be his bride. The king would give us a year and a day to find the recipe."

"Ooooh!" gasped the second lady-mouse. "How exciting!"

A year and a day later, the mouse-king ordered everyone to gather in his palace kitchen and asked who had found the recipe.

A few mice tried, but nothing tasted good, then a small grey lady-mouse stepped forward. "I can make the soup. Will someone set the kettle on the fire? Pour the water in – quite full… now we wait until the water comes to the boil… there, I throw in my sausage skewer…  and now will the mouse-king kindly dip his tail into the boiling water and stir it round? The longer the king stirs it, the stronger the soup will become. Nothing more is needed, only to stir it."

"Can't anyone else do this?" asked the mouse-king nervously, looking at the boiling water.

"No," said the lady-mouse firmly. "The power is contained in your tail alone."

So the mouse-king stood close to the kettle and carefully put out his tail — closer, closer, closer… His tail had only just touched the hot steam when he sprang away from it, exclaiming, "Oh, certainly, you must be my queen! And the soup is so special that we won't make it now, we will save it for our fiftieth wedding anniversary!"

Very soon the wedding took place. But many of the mice, as they were returning home, said that the soup could not be properly called 'soup from a sausage skewer', but should be called 'soup from a mouse's tail'.

What do you think?

Good Luck can Lie in a Button

There was a man who was born into a very poor family. He was an umbrella-maker, but he scarcely made any money. One day when the wind blew a branch down from his pear tree, he carved little pears out of the wood.

The next time he made an umbrella, he used a little wooden pear instead of a button to do up the umbrella. People liked the pear buttons so he made more, and his umbrellas sold like hot cakes! From this time on he was always happy and said: "Good luck may lie in a button."

What is important is that you remember your good luck can lie anywhere. I hope you find it one day...

Grandma's Christmas Gifts

Grandma Burns sat knitting one morning. It was nearly Christmas, and the snow lay deep on the ground. She heard little sobs outside her door and found Peter and Jimmy Rice, two poor boys, crying.

"What can be the matter?" asked Grandma.

"We haven't any sleds!" sighed Jimmy.

"Why, boys can't have a good time without sleds," said Grandma, cheerily. "Let us see if we can't find something."

Grandma found a tray and a large metal pot, and sent the happy boys away. Then all that day she knitted faster than ever — for she was planning something now. That evening, she went to see the carpenter. He promised to make two small sleds in return for the pair of socks she was knitting.

On the night before Christmas she tied the sleds to Peter and Jimmy's door, and then went home, laughing all the way.

The Goose Girl at the Well

One morning, a count met an old woman in a forest. She was struggling to carry two baskets full of fruit. He helped her with them even though they felt as if they were getting heavier and heavier the further they went.

When they reached the old woman's hut, an ugly girl with dull eyes and lank hair came out to meet them. The old woman explained that the girl looked after her geese. Then the old woman gave the count a box made of a single emerald to thank him for his help.

The count thanked her and left, but soon got lost in the forest, wandering for hours. Towards evening he found himself at a castle. Luckily the king and queen who lived there allowed him to spend the night. In return the count offered them the box.

The queen was delighted with the gift, but on opening the box, she fainted!

When she had recovered, she explained, "I had a daughter who was so beautiful that she cried pearls instead of tears. But one day the king got angry and banished her. Inside this box is a pearl just like the ones my daughter cried! Where did you get it?"

So the count told the queen all about the old woman and the goose girl. The next day, they set out to find the hut and as they approached it they saw the goose girl by the well. She began to wash herself — and how different she looked! Her eyes were like stars and her golden hair like sunbeams. The goose girl hugged her parents, who were weeping with joy. "Your daughter has a pure heart — yet you threw her out," the old woman scolded. The king said he would spend the rest of his days making it up to his daughter, and they all lived happily ever after.

The Frogs who Wanted a King

Once upon a time, there was a group of frogs that lived in a marshy swamp. Every day, the frogs went splashing about, without a care in the world. Some weren't happy though, and they thought that they should have a king. So they prayed to the great god Zeus. "Mighty Zeus," they cried, "please send a king to rule us!"

So Zeus sent them a log. For a short while they were happy, but then they prayed to Zeus again, and said to him, "Please send us a king — not just a log, but a real king who will really rule over us."

This irritated Zeus, so he sent a big stork that soon gobbled up most of the frogs. The few that survived wished they hadn't asked for a king in the first place!

Better no rule, than cruel rule.

Anansi and his Wife

Anansi the tricksy spider had a wife who loved to eat lots of food. Anansi was greedy and hated to share, so he prayed to God to give him a new wife with no mouth upon her face. The next day, the new wife arrived. Her face had eyes, a nose, but no mouth. Anansi was delighted when his wife cooked a delicious meal and he ate all of it himself.

But the next day, Anansi realized lots of food was missing. Who could be eating it? He peeped in at the kitchen and saw his wife lift up her arm and poke food into a mouth in her armpit. The mouth ate and ate. Anansi went back to God to complain. "You prayed for a wife with no mouth on her face," said God. "And that's what I gave you."

The Lark and her Young Ones

In early springtime one year, a lark made her nest in the stalks of some young wheat. She laid a clutch of tiny eggs and looked after her chicks tenderly once they had hatched.

One day, the owner of the field came to look over his crop, which was now fully grown and ripe. "The wheat is ready," he said. "I must ask my neighbours to help me with the harvest."

One of the young larks heard his words and told his mother. "Don't worry, my son," she urged. "He's not going to do anything straight away."

And it was indeed a few days before the owner came back again. By this time, though, the wheat was over-ripe. "I must come myself tomorrow with my men," said the owner.

The mother lark heard these words herself and said, "Now it is time to be off, for the man is in earnest — he no longer trusts his friends, but will reap the field himself."

Depend on yourself more than others.

How the Lame Man and the Blind Man Helped Each Other

Two poor men were invited to a feast at the king's palace. One of the men was blind, while the other could not walk. "What a pity it is," said the blind man, "that we cannot go, for we would have enough to eat and drink for once. But I am blind and cannot see the way, and you are lame and cannot walk."

"Take my advice," said the lame man, "and we can both go. You carry me, and I'll show you the way to go."

"A fine idea," said the blind man. So he took the lame man on his back and trudged along to the palace, and both enjoyed the king's feast after all!

Goldilocks and the Three Bears

Once upon a time there was a girl called Goldilocks, who wandered far from home. She came across a cottage, and as the door was open, she went inside. On the table were three bowls of porridge – a big one, a middle-sized one and a little one. Goldilocks tasted them all. The big bowl was too cold, the middle-sized bowl was too hot. The little one was just right, so she ate it all.

By the fire were three chairs. Goldilocks sat in each of them. The big one was too high, the middle-sized one was too low. The little one was just right, but as she stood up from it, it broke.

Next, she went upstairs and found three beds – a big one, a middle-sized one and a little one. The big bed was too hard. The middle-sized one was too soft. The little one was just right, and Goldilocks was soon fast asleep.

Now, the cottage belonged to three bears, and as

soon as they arrived home they knew that someone had been inside. Father Bear growled, "Someone has been eating my porridge."

Mother Bear grumbled, "Someone has been eating my porridge."

And Baby Bear gasped, "Someone has been eating my porridge – and it's all gone!"

Next, Father Bear growled, "Someone has been sitting in my chair."

Mother Bear grumbled, "Someone has been sitting in my chair."

And Baby Bear gasped, "Someone has been sitting in my chair, and has broken it!"

Then the bears went upstairs. Father Bear growled, "Someone has been sleeping in my bed."

Mother Bear grumbled, "Someone has been sleeping in my bed."

And Baby Bear gasped, "Someone has been sleeping in my bed, and they're still there!"

At that Goldilocks woke up with a start! She ran down the stairs, and out of the door until she found herself back home.

The Stolen Axe

Awoodcutter went out one morning to cut some firewood, and discovered that his favourite axe was missing. He couldn't find it anywhere! He was looking around when he noticed his neighbour's son standing near the woodshed. The woodcutter thought, "Aha! That boy must have stolen my axe. Look at the guilty look on his face. I can't prove it, but he MUST have stolen my axe."

A few days later the woodcutter was surprised to come across his own axe under a pile of firewood. "I remember now," he said, "It's just where I left it!"

The next time he saw his neighbour's son, the woodcutter looked at the boy. 'How odd,' he thought, 'somehow this boy has lost his guilty look.' Which just goes to show that we see in people what we want to see…

The Fortune Teller

There was once a man who sat in the market place and told fortunes. People loved to hear what was going to happen in their future – even if it was bad news – so he was kept busy every day.

One morning, however, a boy suddenly pushed through the crowds and shouted that the fortune teller's house had been broken into by thieves. They had made off with everything they could lay their hands on! The fortune teller jumped up at once and rushed off, cursing the thieves.

A bystander chuckled to himself and said, "Our friend claims to know what is going to happen to others, but he's not clever enough to see what's in store for himself."

Only follow those who lead by example, not by empty words.

The Country Fellow and the River

A **country boy** was sent to market by his mother to sell butter and cheese, but on his way he came to a fast-flowing river. The boy laid himself down on the bank to wait until the water ran out.

He waited all day long but it was no good — the water would not stop! About midnight, he gave up and went home, taking all his market goods back with him. "Why, what's this?" said his mother, when he returned. "You haven't sold a thing?"

"Well Mother, I came across a river that ran all day long, so I sat till just now waiting for it to run out — but it is running still!"

"My son," said the woman, "You and I will be laid in the grave before the river runs dry. You will never sell your butter and cheese if you wait for that!"

Foundling

A huntsman was walking in the woods when he came across a baby boy. The huntsman called him Foundling, and brought him up as his own child with his daughter, Lina. They were very happy together until one day, Lina heard their cook, who was a witch, planning to kill Foundling.

Lina told Foundling that they had to run away, so they packed their bags and left — but the witch chased after them. When they heard her footsteps, Foundling changed himself into a rose bush and Lina became a rose. The witch ran past but when they changed back she came after them again. This time Foundling turned himself into a pond and Lina became a duck. The witch stopped at the pond to take a drink and as she leaned over the water, the duck seized her hair and tugged her into the water! The old witch sank to the bottom of the pond and the children escaped.

The Shepherdess and the Chimney-sweep

There was once a sitting room in which there stood a wooden cupboard, decorated with beautiful carvings. In the middle was a little man with a long beard, two tiny horns and legs like a goat. The children of the house called him Billy Goat's-legs.

On a table nearby stood a little china shepherdess. At her side stood a chimney sweep, also made of china. He and the shepherdess were in love.

Another china figure stood on the table – an old Chinaman who could nod his head. He acted as the shepherdess's father, always telling her what to do.

One day, Billy Goat's-legs asked if the little shepherdess would marry him. The Chinaman nodded his head, but the sheperdess said to the chimney sweep, "I won't marry him. I don't want to. Let's run away."

They climbed down to the floor, but just then, Billy Goat's-legs noticed them escaping. "They are getting away!" he shouted, and the Chinaman started to chase them.

"Quick, up the chimney!" said the chimney sweep. Up and up and up they climbed, and at long last they were out on the roof.

"I never dreamed that the world was so huge," cried the shepherdess. "Please, take me back."

So the couple climbed back down the chimney and saw the Chinaman lying on the floor with his head broken off! He had fallen off the table as he chased them.

"Don't worry," said the chimney sweep, "he can be glued back together." And they climbed up the table and stood in their old places.

The very next day, the Chinaman was fixed and put back next to them as good as new, except he could no longer nod his head. So later on, when Billy Goat's-legs called out again, asking for the shepherdess's hand in marriage, the Chinaman did not nod in agreement. And so the little shepherdess and the chimney sweep lived happily ever after.

Which was the King?

King Henry the Fourth of France was hunting in a large forest one day. Towards evening he told his men to ride home along the main road while he went a different, longer route back to the palace.

As the king rode along he saw a child.

"Well, my boy," said the king, "are you looking for your father?"

"No, sir," answered the boy. "I am looking for the king. They say he is hunting in the woods, and may ride out this way. I'm waiting to see him."

"Oh, if that is what you wish," said King Henry, "get up behind me on my horse and I'll take you to see him."

The boy got up at once, and sat behind the king. The horse trotted briskly along, while the king and the boy became acquainted. "They say that the king always has a number of men with him," said the boy, "how will I know which one is King Henry?"

"That will be easy," was the answer. "All the other men will take off their hats, but the king will keep his on."

"Do you mean that the one with his hat on will be the king?"

"Certainly," said the king.

Soon they came to the main road where the king's men were waiting. They seemed amused when they saw the boy, and as the horse rode by, they greeted the king by taking off their hats.

"Well, my boy," said King Henry, "which do you think is the king?"

"I don't know," answered the boy, "but it must be either you or me, for we both have our hats on."

The Sea-hare

Once upon a time there was a princess who had a tower with twelve windows. The windows looked out in every direction of her kingdom, and when she gazed through them, nothing could be kept secret from her.

The princess had declared she would only marry a man who could hide where she couldn't find him. She thought this was an impossible task, and soon many men were imprisoned for trying and failing.

Then one day, a young man begged her to let him have three tries. As she liked the look of him, she said yes. He thought for a long time about how he should hide, then went out hunting. He was about to fire at a raven, when the bird cried, "Don't shoot – I'll help you if you spare me." The young man decided to let him go.

Next, he aimed at a fish – but the fish cried, "Don't shoot, and I'll reward you." Again, the young man agreed.

Finally he aimed at a fox, but the fox also promised to help so he too went free.

The very next day when the young

man had to hide himself from the princess, he asked the raven for help. The raven fetched an egg, cut it in half, and shut the youth inside. The princess took a long time searching for the man but finally she saw the egg moving, and found him.

The day after, the fish swallowed the man, and went down to the bottom of the lake to hide him. The princess eventually saw the bulge in the fish's stomach. On the last day, he met the fox. "Where shall I hide myself?" he asked. "That's hard," answered the fox. But he changed the man into a small sea-hare, and himself into a stallholder.

The princess came to the market, and bought the sea-hare. The fox told him to creep under her hair when she went to the window. And so the youth did. The princess went to every window, and did not see the man. The princess admitted she was beaten and the youth changed to his real shape. The princess agreed to the wedding (she didn't mind, to tell you the truth) and they lived happily ever after.

The Eagle and the Kite

An eagle and a kite were perched in the branches of a tree together. The eagle was very sad because he couldn't find a mate, so the kite said to him, "Why not take me? I would be a good match. In fact, I am much stronger than you. I have often carried away a fully grown ostrich in my talons."

The eagle was impressed by these words and agreed to the match.

Then, one day the eagle said to his new wife, "Why don't you fly off and bring me back an ostrich?"

The kite soared into the air, but when she returned, all she brought back was a straggly mouse. "Is this," said the eagle, "the fulfilment of your promise to me?"

The kite replied, "In order to obtain your royal hand in marriage, there is nothing that I would not have promised."

Do not trust everything people say.

Saving the Bell

The foolish men of Gotham heard that invaders were coming to attack, so they decided to hide their precious church bell.

"Where shall we hide it?" they asked,

Someone said, "Let's sink it in our pond."

So they rowed to the middle of the pond and pushed the bell overboard.

"The bell is safe from the enemy, but how will we be able to find it again?" they wondered.

"That's easy," one of them said. "All we have to do is mark where we dropped it in!"

So they took a knife and carved a mark in the side of their boat. "It was right here that we heaved the bell out," said one man, proudly.

Then they rowed back to the shore, pleased that they would be able to find their bell by the mark on the side of their boat.

The Cheeses that Ran Away

A man from Gotham filled a sack with cheese and started off to market. When he sat down to rest, one cheese slipped out of the sack and rolled all the way down the hill.

"Ah!" said the man, "So you can run to market, can you? Well then, if you can go to market alone, so can the others."

So he emptied his bag, and as the cheeses rolled away he shouted, "Meet me at the market place!"

Most of the cheeses ended up in the bushes, but the man went cheerfully to the market, thinking he would meet them there. Of course the cheeses weren't at the market, so the man said, "I did think they were running too fast. Maybe they went too far."

SEPTEMBER

The Fox and the Tiger

A young tiger was out hunting one day when he came across a fox. He was just about to pounce on it when the fox spoke up. "Tiger, you must not think that you are really the king of beasts. Follow me along the road and see what happens — if people aren't frightened when they see me, then you may swallow me in one gulp."

The tiger smiled, and said he was willing to do as the fox said, so they walked along a highway where there were lots of travellers. When the people saw the tiger in the distance, they screamed and ran away. "Ah ha!" The crafty fox said, "Everyone is scared of me! You should be too."

So the tiger turned and ran, never realizing that the people had been wary of him all along.

The Jackdaw
and the Doves

One day a jackdaw noticed some doves living in a warm, safe dovecote, and saw that they were given food each day by their owner. He wished for an easy life too, so he painted himself white and asked the doves to let him in.

The doves were fooled by his disguise, and agreed that he could live with them. The jackdaw was silent, so he wouldn't give himself away by his harsh cry. However, one day he forgot himself and began to chatter. The doves kicked him out at once.

The jackdaw returned to his own kind but because he was white, his friends failed to recognize him and they too turned him away. So in trying to win favour with two sets of birds, he ended up gaining neither.

If you try to be all things to all people, you may well please no one — not even yourself.

Five Peas in a Pod

There were once five peas in a pod on a pea plant. As the pod grew, the peas grew with it until one day – *crack!* The five peas rolled out into a little boy's palm. He wanted them for his peashooter, and he soon shot them, one after another. One of the peas landed high up in a mossy crack under the attic window of a little house and took root.

Inside the attic was a tiny flat where a poor woman lived with her daughter. The girl was very ill and her mother was so worried about her. When Spring came, the mother opened the curtains early one morning and the girl cried, "What is that green thing peeping in at the window?"

"Oh!" said her mother. "A little pea has taken root and is growing green leaves. Now you have your own little garden."

The woman drew the sick girl's bed closer to the window, so she could see the plant. When the woman returned in the evening, her daughter said, "Mother, the little pea is growing so well, I feel I too will get better soon."

This made the woman very happy indeed. She carefully tied a piece of string for the pea tendrils to climb as they grew.

The sick girl watched the plant growing bigger every day. She even began to manage to sit herself up. One morning her mother announced, "There's a flower coming!"

The girl now had the strength to stand up and kiss the pink pea blossom that was opening. She was so happy, it felt like her birthday. And it was this show of strength that made the woman believe that her sick daughter would one day be well again.

Anansi and the Turtle

Anansi the spider had just baked some delicious yams when he heard a knock at the door. It was Turtle, come for a visit. Now, Anansi didn't want to share his yams with anybody so he came up with a plan. Just as Turtle sat down, Anansi yelled, "Turtle, your hands are dirty! Please go and wash them." Turtle slowly crawled to the river, washed his hands, then slowly crawled back.

Meanwhile Anansi was eating the yams and by the time Turtle got back, they were half gone. Just as Turtle sat down, Anansi yelled again, "Turtle, your hands are still dirty! Go and wash them again!"

Poor turtle did as Anansi asked, and by the time Turtle had crawled back, there wasn't a single yam left!

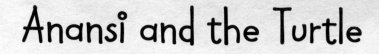

Reynard Steals Fish

One day Reynard the fox saw a man driving a cart full of fish, and as he was very hungry the sight made his mouth water. Quick as a flash he lay down in the road, and played dead. The driver saw him there, and said, "That will make a beautiful fox fur scarf."

He got down from the cart, grabbed Reynard and threw him into the back along with the fish. Then he went driving on as before. Quick as lightning, Reynard threw all the fish out of the cart, then he jumped out himself, and enjoyed the best meal he had in weeks. The man didn't notice any of this, and drove all the way home. When he arrived at the door he called out, "Ann, come and see what I have got!"

But when his wife looked into the cart she said, "Well, you seem to have brought me nothing!"

Hop-toads and Pearls

A bad-tempered, mean old widow once had two daughters. The eldest was just like her mother while the youngest, her stepdaughter, was kind.

The stepdaughter was made to do all the chores, and it was her job to fetch the water every day from a distant well. One day when she had filled her bucket, an old woman who was passing asked her for a drink. "Yes, of course," the stepdaughter replied, and she held the bucket carefully for her.

Now, this was not really an old peasant, but a fairy. "I will reward your kindness," she said. "Every time you speak, a pearl shall fall from your mouth."

When the girl reached home later that day her stepmother scolded her for being late. "I'm sorry," the girl replied. As she spoke a pearl dropped from her lips.

The widow made a grab for the falling pearl and bit into it. "It's real!" she gasped, in amazement.

The girl told her story, and the greedy stepmother immediately called her eldest daughter to her and said, "Go and get water from the well, and if anyone asks you for a drink, make sure you give it!"

The eldest daughter grumpily did as she was told. When she was at the well, the same old woman passed by and asked for a drink. The girl agreed but did not help her. So the fairy said, "I will make you a gift to equal your rudeness. Every time you speak, a toad shall come from your mouth."

"Well, daughter, what happened?" cried the mother eagerly when she returned.

When the daughter opened her mouth to answer, two toads sprang from it!

The old widow was so cross that she threw her kind stepdaughter out of the house! Luckily she fell in love with a prince and lived happily ever after. As for the widow and her daughter, they were miserable for the rest of their toad-filled days.

The Cage-bird and the Bat

A caged bird longed for the skies she could see through the bars, and even though she no longer had the joy of flying, she sang with the most beautiful voice – but she sang at night, when everyone was asleep.

One night, a bat clung to the bars of the cage, and asked the bird why she sang only at night. "I have a good reason," said the bird. "It was when I was singing in the daytime that a birdcatcher heard my voice, and caught me. Since then I have only sung at night."

But the bat replied, "It is no use doing that now, when you are a prisoner. If only you had done so before you were caught, you might still be free."

Precautions are useless after the event.

The Nail

After a good day's business at a fair, a tradesman was about to set out for home on his horse, when a stable-boy said to him, "Sir, a nail is missing in the shoe on the left hind foot."

"Leave it for now," replied the tradesman, "I am in a hurry."

He rode off but his horse soon began to limp, and from limping it came to stumbling, and presently the beast fell down and broke its leg. The man had to leave his poor horse lying by the road and continue on foot through the woods. When he was still five miles from home, a gang of robbers stole all his money. He didn't reach his house until very late at night. "And all this misfortune," said he to himself, "is owing to the lack of a nail. Next time, more care, less speed!

Jack and the Beanstalk

Jack and his mother were very poor, so they decided to sell their only cow at the market. But on his way, Jack met a funny little man who offered him five magic beans in exchange for his cow. Jack took the beans at once, gave the man the cow, and ran off home to his mother, but she scolded him and flung the beans out of the window.

The next morning Jack awoke to find the most enormous beanstalk growing where the beans had fallen. It had grown right past his bedroom window and reached up into the clouds.

Without any hesitation Jack began to climb the beanstalk. When he reached the top he came to a vast castle, so he knocked at the door. It was opened by a huge woman, who said, "My husband eats boys so you'd better hide." She bundled Jack into a cupboard just as a giant man came into the kitchen.

"Fee fi fo fum! I smell the blood of an Englishman!" he roared.

"Don't be silly, dear," said the giant's wife. The giant then poured out a bag of gold onto the table, counted all the coins and put them back in the bag. Then he fell asleep and at once Jack darted out of the cupboard, grabbed the bag of gold and climbed down the beanstalk as fast as he could. His mother bought two cows with the money.

After a while Jack decided he wanted to climb the beanstalk again. The giant's wife was not pleased to see him.

"My husband lost a bag of gold when you were here," she muttered, and then the ground began to shake. Jack hid in the cupboard again as the giant stomped in.

"Fee fi fo fum! I smell the blood of an Englishman!" he roared.

"Don't be silly, dear," said the giant's wife. The giant then lifted a golden hen onto the table, and the hen laid a golden egg. With a smile on his big face the giant fell asleep. Quick as a flash, Jack darted out of the cupboard, grabbed the golden hen and climbed quickly down the beanstalk.

Jack's mother bought a herd of cows with the golden eggs that the hen soon laid, and as before they were very happy. But after a while Jack decided to climb the beanstalk one last time. When Jack arrived at the castle this time he hid under the table just as the giant entered the kitchen. "Fee fi fo fum! I smell the blood of an Englishman!"

"Look in the cupboard," said the giant's wife, but the cupboard was empty. The giant then took out a golden harp, and said, "Play!"

The harp played so sweetly that the giant was soon fast asleep. Jack crept out from under the table and grabbed it, but the harp called out, "Master!" The giant awoke and chased Jack, who scrambled down the beanstalk with the harp in his arms. As soon as Jack reached the ground he grabbed an axe and chopped through the beanstalk. The giant crashed to the ground — and that was the end of him. Jack and his mother lived happily for the rest of their days.

The Little Folks' Presents

Long ago, two men were travelling when they heard some beautiful music. They followed the sound and found a crowd of tiny people dancing. As the two men approached, a tiny old man leapt up and shaved their heads! Then he told them to help themselves to a pile of coal as they left. To the travellers' amazement, the next morning when they woke up, their hair had grown back and the coal had turned to lumps of pure gold!

Now, one of the men was greedy and wanted more gold. So he went back the next night. This time he filled two sacks with coal. But when he awoke the next day all his gold had vanished and he was still bald. Luckily his friend was kind and shared his wealth, but the greedy man's hair never grew back!

How the Camel got his Hump

In the beginning, when the world was so new-and-all, and the animals were just beginning to work, there was a camel that lived in the middle of a howling desert. He refused to help, and when anybody spoke to him, he just said, "Humph!"

The horse, the dog and the ox all came to him and said, "Come and work like the rest of us."

"Humph!" said the camel.

At the end of the day, the man called the horse and the dog and the ox together, and said, "Friends, I'm sorry but that humph-thing won't work, so you will have to do extra."

That made the three animals very angry (with the world being so new-and-all).

Presently the djinn in charge of All Deserts, came rolling along in a cloud of dust.

"Djinn," said the horse, "is it right for anyone to be idle, and not work?"

"Certainly not," said the djinn. So they told him about the camel.

"Very good," said the djinn. "I'll humph *him* if you will kindly wait a minute." And he found the camel in the middle of the howling desert.

"You've given the others extra work ever since Monday morning," said the djinn.

"Humph!" said the camel.

"I shouldn't say that again if I were you," said the djinn. But the camel said "Humph!" once more. Straightaway his back began puffing up into a great big lolloping humph!

"Do you *see* that?" said the djinn. "That's your very own humph that you've brought upon yourself. You will be able to work now for three days without eating, because you can live on your humph."

And from that day to this the camel has worn a humph (we call it a 'hump' now) – but he still hasn't learned how to behave.

The Foolish Shepherd

There once was a foolish boy who took a job as a shepherd. Everyone said he was too stupid for the work, but the farmer said anyone could guard sheep. "All you have to do," he said, "is watch the the herd, and if a wolf comes, pick up a big stone like this," he picked up a stone to show him, "then throw it to scare the wolf away. Do you understand?"

The boy said he did and just a few hours later, a wolf did appear. The boy looked at the stones on the ground, but there wasn't one just like the stone the farmer had shown him! He ran all the way back to the farm to get one but when he came back all the flock were scattered or killed!

After that the farmer admitted that even shepherds need some brains.

The Donkey Carrying the Statue

Long ago in a far-off city there was a procession to the temple of an important goddess. The statue of the goddess was carried at the front on the back of a donkey, surrounded by priests and priestesses and followed by hundreds of slaves chanting prayers and throwing rose petals.

As the donkey passed along, crowds of people bowed low in front of the statue he carried. The foolish donkey thought the people were bowing their heads to him. He bristled with pride, puffed out his chest, threw his head back and refused to move another step. At once the driver gave him a sharp tap with the whip, shouting, "You idiot! Do you think the people are worshipping you?"

It is not a wise move to take the credit due to other people.

Work Hard and Do Well

A young boy called Abdul grew up believing that you can do anything if you work hard enough. One day, after he glimpsed the princess of his kingdom in her carriage, he went to the palace to ask for her hand in marriage. 'For,' he thought, 'Success comes to he who asks for it.'

"Oh Caliph," he began, "I beg you to let me marry your daughter!" The whole court laughed at the thought of a simple village boy marrying their princess, and some said he should be punished. But the Caliph spoke kindly to the boy and declared, "Ages ago a ruby of great value was lost in the Tigris. He who finds it shall have the hand of my daughter."

Abdul was pleased to hear this and went to the shores of the Tigris. Every morning, day after day, he worked to drain the river so he could search its bed. The fishes in the river at last became fearful that he might take all their water away, and they came before their king to ask for his help.

"Why is he doing this?' asked the fish king.

"He wants the king's ruby that lies buried in the bottom of the Tigris," was the reply.

"I advise you, then," said the fish king, "to give it to him. For if he is determined to find it, and has a strong will, he will work until he has drained the last drop of water from the Tigris."

So the next day, the fishes threw the ruby into Abdul's bucket, and he took it to the Caliph. The Caliph kept his promise and agreed that the princess could be his wife.

The Spirit in the Bottle

A poor woodcutter and his son were working hard in the forest one day when the boy found an old bottle. Inside was a strange creature spinning. "Let me out!" it cried.

The boy drew the cork out of the bottle and as he did so the creature swelled until it became a mighty spirit. "Here is your reward for releasing me," it boomed, and the spirit gave the boy a sticking plaster. "Put one end of the plaster on any wound and it will heal. Put the other end over steel and it will change into silver." Then the spirit vanished for good.

The woodcutter was thrilled by his son's good fortune, as it meant he could afford to go to school and study. And because the boy could heal all wounds with his magic plaster, he became the most famous doctor in the whole world.

The Farmer and the Fox

There was once a farmer who was bothered by a fox, which came prowling around his farmyard every night. Each morning, the farmer awoke to find yet more of his chickens, ducks or geese had been carried off.

The farmer set a trap and caught the fox. As a punishment, he tied a bunch of dry brushwood to the fox's tail and set fire to it.

The terrified creature ran off, trying to escape from the fire burning at its tail. However, the fox made straight for the farmer's fields, where the corn 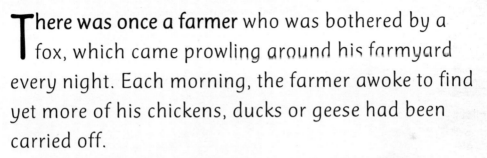 was standing ripe and ready for cutting. As the fox ran through the corn, it quickly caught fire, and the farmer's harvest was destroyed.

Revenge is a double-edged sword.

The Flower Princess

There once was a princess who had been put under a strange enchantment. She transformed into a flower each day, regaining her own shape at night. Her husband knew that the only way to break the spell would be to pick her while she was a flower — but how could he know which one was her?

One morning, when the princess once again transformed into a flower the prince hastened to the field where she would be growing — a thought had come to him. He looked closely at every flower. Finally he stopped before a cornflower and plucked it. All at once his princess stood before him.

"How could you tell it was me?" she asked.

"All the other flowers had stood in the field all night so they had dew on them," he replied, "while you alone had none."

The Donkey and the Mule

A **man who owned a donkey** and a mule loaded them up one day and set off on a long journey.

The donkey found the long walk hard going. On the verge of collapse, he begged the mule to carry part of his load — but the mule refused. At last, the donkey could take no more. He stumbled and crumpled on the ground. The owner now had the problem of how to carry on with his journey. At last, he did the only thing possible — he piled the donkey's load on top of the mule's.

The mule could only just manage the extra weight, and, as it staggered painfully along, it said, "I have only got what I deserve — if I had helped the donkey, I would not be carrying so much."

Prevention is better than cure.

Cap o' Rushes

A rich gentleman decided to ask his daughter how much she loved him one morning.

"I love you as fresh meat loves salt," she replied.

"Why, then you don't love me at all!" her father said, furiously. Then he ordered her to leave his house and never return.

The poor girl left her home and wandered until she came to a great house. To cover up her fine clothes she made some rushes into a hooded cloak, then she knocked at the door to ask if they needed a maid. "I ask no wages," she said, "and will do any sort of work."

They said she could stay and wash the dishes, if she wished. The girl agreed, but she didn't tell them her name. They called her 'Cap o' Rushes' after her strange reed cloak.

After a short while it was announced that a dance was to be held at the palace, and the servants were to be invited. On the night, Cap o' Rushes said that she was too tired to go, but when the others had left she took off her cloak and went to the dance.

Well, who should be there but her master's son, and what should he do but fall in love with her? He would dance with no one else all evening and even gave her a ring as a token of his affection.

The next day the master's son tried to find the girl he had danced with, but no one knew who she was! He soon grew so lovesick that he had to stay in bed, and was quite miserable.

When Cap o' Rushes heard of his state she decided to make him some soup. She slipped the ring into it before the cook took it upstairs. When the young man drank it he saw the ring at the bottom and exclaimed, "Send me whoever made this soup!"

Cap o' Rushes went to the prince, and took off her cloak. He recognized her staightaway and asked her to marry him.

Everyone was asked to the wedding – even Cap o' Rushes' father. She served his dishes without salt in them, and he realized how wrong he was to mind her answer. She forgave him, and they all lived happily ever after.

The Boy and the Filberts

One morning a boy noticed a jar of nuts, or filberts, on a shelf. They looked so tasty that he couldn't resist reaching up and lifting it down. He thrust his hand inside the jar, and greedily grasped as many of the nuts he could hold.

But he couldn't get his hand out of the jar, for the neck was too small to allow such a large handful to get through. The little boy didn't want to let go of all his tasty treats, but unless he did, he wouldn't be able to get his hand out.

Just as he burst into tears of frustration a neighbour passed by the window and saw what the trouble was. "There, there," she said. "Don't be greedy. If you can be content with half of what you have, you'll be able to get your hand out easily enough."

Do not attempt too much at once.

The Toad

A family of toads lived at the bottom of a deep, dark well. They were very content except for the youngest toad. He felt a terrible longing to go and explore the outside world, so one day he climbed out of the well and hopped down the road into a garden.

There he met a stork who told him about the countries she had visited — especially the warm land of Egypt, where she went in winter. It sounded very exciting.

"I must get to Egypt!" the little toad said to himself. And off he hopped to see as much of the world as he could...

I do not know if the little toad ever made it to Egypt — or indeed what happened to him. But I do know that he had the longing to explore and learn — and it shone most brightly within him.

Simple Hans and the Slap

Simple Hans was in the market place when a man mistook Hans for someone else and slapped him. Hans reported the man to the judge and demanded that he be punished.

The judge and the man turned out to be old friends. Laughing, the judge told the man to pay Hans just one penny for the slap. The man chuckled and went on his way – without paying.

Hans was furious. He went back to the judge and asked, "Are you telling me the fine for a slap is just one penny?" When the judge said it was, Hans slapped the judge on the face! Then he said, "You may have my penny when your friend comes back with it."

The Wolf in Sheep's Clothing

There was once a wolf who kept trying to steal sheep from a flock. The shepherd and sheepdogs were very watchful and always chased the wolf away, but the wolf did not give up. He hung around, waiting for a chance.

An opportunity came one day when he found a sheepskin that had been cast aside. He put it over his coat and tied it around him, so he was quite disguised. Then he strolled among the sheep — none of them noticed anything strange. In fact, the lamb of the sheep whose skin the wolf was wearing began to follow the wolf.

Leading the lamb away from the flock, the wolf made a meal of her. And for some time afterwards, he succeeded in deceiving the sheep and the shepherd and enjoyed many good meals.

Appearances can be deceptive.

The Princess
and the Raven

A king was lost in a forest one evening. As he wandered, he came across a great raven perched on a branch. The raven offered to guide the king home, on the condition that he could marry the king's daughter. At first the king refused, horrified, but in the end he had to promise — for he could see no way out of the forest

The raven led him home then said, "Tomorrow I will come for my bride."

Sure enough, in the morning there was the raven perched upon the castle gate.

But it was not the princess he was given — for the king sent his shepherd's daughter instead. The raven offered the girl a golden goblet of red wine, a silver cup of white wine, and an earthenware jug full of bitter beer. She took a good drink of the beer, and by that the raven knew she was no princess. He sent her away and demanded the real princess.

The next day, the king sent his steward's daughter. She took the white wine, when it was offered to her — and the raven knew by this that he had been tricked again.

"Tomorrow morning," said the raven to the king, "I will come for the true princess, and if I don't get her I will tear your castle down about your ears!"

The king was now terribly frightened so the next day his daughter — the true princess — set out to see the raven. The raven offered her a drink and she chose the golden goblet of red wine. As she did so the raven changed into a handsome prince.

"You have freed me!" he said. "I was under a spell that could only be broken when a real princess drank from the golden goblet."

So the pair married, and they lived happily ever after.

The Sun and the Moon

In the beginning the Sun and the Moon quarrelled with each other often. The Sun said, "You are only the Moon and are not much good. If I did not give you light, you would be no good at all."

But the Moon answered, "You are only the Sun, and you are very hot. The women like me better, for when I shine at night, they go outdoors and spin."

These words of the Moon made the Sun so angry that it threw sand in the Moon's face, and you can still see the dark spots on the face of the Moon.

Arachne the Weaver

There was once a little Greek girl called Arachne who was so proud of her weaving that she boasted she could even beat the Goddess Athena at it. Her friends warned her it was dangerous to say she was better than a goddess but she was so sure of herself she didn't stop. One day an old woman warned her, "Do you really mean what you say?"

"Of course," she replied. "My weaving beats everyone."

In a flash the old woman disappeared and the mighty goddess stood in her place. "Very well," she said, "Let us have a competition."

Arachne wove a web of marvellous beauty but when Athena's turn came, her weaving was so fine it nearly floated away. Arachne was beaten, and as a punishment Athena turned her into a spider so she would spend the rest of her life weaving.

The Beggar's Dream

Once upon a time there was a poor beggar who was very thin and hungry. One day, a friend asked him why he looked so sad.

"Ah, I had a dream," the beggar replied.

"A good dream, or a bad one?" asked his friend.

"A bit of both. I dreamt I was invited to the palace of the king. The walls were hung with silk and the cushions stuffed with down. His majesty himself offered me a plate of meat. Would I have cold ham, he asked, or a hot roast chicken?

I asked for the chicken. Well, the king went away to see about it being cooked and while he was gone, I woke up. And now I'm kicking myself I didn't ask for the ham."

The Owl and the Birds

An owl advised the rest of the birds that whenever they noticed a little shoot growing from an acorn, they should pull it up out of the ground. The owl said that acorns encouraged the mistletoe to grow, from which hunters could make sticky bird-lime. The hunters would then paste the bird-lime onto reeds, which they would place in trees, bushes and hedgerows. Then birds would get stuck to the reeds and be caught by the hunters.

The birds all thought that the owl had gone mad, and took no notice of these words of warning. Afterwards, many of them found out the hard way that her words were true. Then they marvelled at her knowledge and decided that she must be the wisest of birds.

But by then it was too late. Now, whenever the birds look up to the owl and ask for her advice, she no longer gives it. She just hangs her head and feels sorry for their earlier stupidity.

Destroy the seed of evil, or it will grow up to be your ruin.

The Windmill

A **long time ago**, there stood a stately windmill on a hill. It had been there as long as anyone could remember and looked rather as if it was growing out of the countryside. The windmill spent its days thinking deeply.

"I am very lucky," it said to itself, "that people like looking at me. To start with, I always have bright eyes. Either the sun's rays or the moonbeams shine at my windows, or the miller lights them up with candles. Out in the world, I can't see anything else like me. I can see houses but they just look wingless and strange.

"I have been here for many years. And I know that the time will arrive when I will become old and tumble down. But I will be built up again, newer and better. I will look different, but as long as I have the miller and his wife living at my heart, and the children running around me like thoughts, I will be the same deep down inside. And everyone will say: 'There's the mill on the hill — what a sight to see.'"

And so the days passed, and the days came, until one afternoon the windmill caught fire and burnt down.

Very luckily, the miller's family had not been at home at the time. They were filled with sadness to lose the old mill, but they soon built a beautiful new mill, even better than the first. And the miller and his wife lived at the heart of the new mill and their little children ran around it like thoughts. Its windows were always brightly lit, and its sails creaked steadily round and round while it stood there, thinking deeply. And everyone said: "There's the mill on the hill — what a sight to see."

The Lion in Love

There was once a lion who fell in love with a girl, so he went to her parents to ask for her hand in marriage. The parents did not wish to give their daughter to the lion, yet they did not want to make him angry either.

At last the father said, "We fear that you might injure our daughter. May we suggest that you have your claws removed and your teeth pulled out. Then we will consider your proposal again."

The lion was so much in love that he did indeed have his claws cut and teeth removed. Then he went again to see the parents, with high hopes that they would agree to the marriage. But this time they just laughed in his face, for now they had no reason to be afraid of him.

Love can tame the wildest.

OCTOBER

The Cloud of Dust

Two men wanted to raise some wild boar for meat, so they went out into the woods to search for some piglets. They soon found a cave with some young boars inside and one man went in to fetch them. He bundled them into a sack, while the other kept watch outside. But all of a sudden the mother boar came charging back, teeth gleaming, tusks ready to slash. The man on watch only had time to grab her tail as she ran into the cave! As she struggled to get free, a great cloud of dust was thrown up into the air. The man inside the cave shouted to his friend, "Where has all the dust come from? I can't see a thing!" The man outside shouted, "If this tail breaks, you'll soon find out what it means!"

The Princess and the Pea

Long ago there was a prince who wanted to get married to a princess. He had been searching for a long time but hadn't found anyone he liked.

Then one evening, during a thunderstorm, there was a knock at the palace door. A girl, claiming to be a princess, was outside in the rain. She asked for shelter for the night and the prince let her in.

The queen didn't trust the girl, however, so she came up with a plan. She placed a pea on the girl's bed and ordered that twenty mattresses be piled on top of it. Only a true princess would feel it!

The next morning the queen asked the girl how she had slept. "Oh, very badly!" the girl sighed. "There was something hard in the bed, and now I am very sore."

The prince – who had fallen in love with the girl as soon as he saw her – was overjoyed that she was a real princess. The two were married and they lived happily ever after.

The Three Dogs

A shepherd set out with his three sheep to seek his fortune. He hadn't travelled far when he came across a man with three dogs. "Will you swap your three sheep for my three dogs?" the man asked. "The smallest one is called Salt, and will bring you food whenever you wish. The second is called Pepper, and he'll fight to protect you, and the big one is called Mustard. He can break iron with his teeth."

The shepherd thought that the dogs sounded very useful, so he swapped. Every day Salt brought him a fine meal, so the shepherd was happy.

A few days later the shepherd came across a carriage with a beautiful girl inside. The coachman told him that a dragon lived nearby, and every year it ate a maiden. This year the king's daughter had been chosen and he was driving her to meet her fate. The shepherd thought for a time, then decided to try and help the poor girl. He set off to find the dragon and waited in its lair. When the dragon appeared the shepherd called, "Pepper, help!"

The loyal dog fought bravely to protect his master and at long last overcame the dragon, and killed it. The princess begged the shepherd to return to her father's castle with her but he told her he wanted to see the world, and would return in three years.

The coach set off without him. However, as soon as they were out of sight, the coachman turned on the princess and said, "Promise to tell your father that I killed the dragon or I will kill you."

The princess had to promise, and she wept when the king said the coachman could marry her as his reward. Each year she begged for the wedding to be put off, until after three years passed the coachman said he would wait no longer.

The shepherd returned on the same day. When he heard of the coachman's lie he protested that it was he  who defeated the dragon. He made such a nuisance of himself that they locked him up in prison. At once he called out, "Mustard, help!" The dog bit through the iron bars and released the shepherd, and he rushed to the church to stop the wedding. The coachman was banished from the kingdom, and the princess and the shepherd were married at last.

The Grasshoppers and the Ants

Day after day the ants were working long hours gathering food to store for the winter, while the grasshoppers did nothing but sit on blades of grass and sing from dawn to dusk.

When winter came, the ants had plenty of food, and the grasshoppers felt the pinch of hunger. After a few days, some grasshoppers went to the ants and begged them for some grains.

The ants asked, "Why didn't you collect a store of food?"

"Well," replied the grasshopper, "we were so busy singing that we didn't have the time."

"If you spent the summer singing," replied the ants, "you'd better spend the winter dancing."

It is best to be prepared in case hard times arrive.

The Farmer's
Favourite Daughter

Once upon a time there was a farmer who had two daughters who were constantly asking him which one of them was his favourite.

"I love you both the same," was always his answer, but they did not accept this, asking, "But which one of us do you love the most?"

Finally he secretly gave them both a blue bead, telling each one that she should tell no one of the gift.

After that whenever either of the daughters asked him, "Which one of us is your favourite?" he would answer, "I love best the one to whom I gave the blue bead," and each one was satisfied with his answer.

The Blind Man and the Cub

There was a blind man who had so fine a sense of touch that when any animal was put into his hands, he could tell exactly what it was merely by feeling it. He could tell a mole from its velvety coat. He could tell a lizard from its scaly skin. He could tell a chick from its fluffy down and a goose from its feathers. One day, a wolf cub was placed in his hands, and he was asked what he thought it was. He felt the cub all over for some time, and then said, "Indeed, I am not sure whether it is a wolf's cub or a fox's, but this I do know — it would never do to trust it in a flock of sheep."

Evil tendencies are shown early.

Straw, Coal and Bean

An old **woman** gathered together a serving of
beans and made a fire on which to cook them.
While she was pouring the beans into the pot, one
fell onto the floor where it met a stray piece of straw
and a lump of coal. They became friends, and
decided to seek their fortunes together. They set off,
and soon came to a small brook. The straw decided
to lie across it, so the others could walk across him.

When the coal got to the middle, the straw caught
fire and fell into the brook. The coal slid in after him.
The bean, who had stayed on the bank, laughed so
hard that he burst!

Luckily a passing tailor sewed him back together.
The bean thanked him and because the tailor used
black thread, all beans now
have a black seam.

Rapunzel

Many years ago a husband and wife were expecting their first baby. They were very poor and often hungry. One morning, the woman looked over her garden wall into her neighbour's vegetable patch. There she saw a bed of delicious-looking salad. She longed for it so much that her husband climbed over to get her some. Unfortunately, their neighbour was an evil witch, and she caught him in the act. The witch would only let the man go if he promised to give up his child when it was born. The man tried and tried to offer the witch anything else but it was no good — when his little daughter was born the witch took her. The witch called her Rapunzel, and imprisoned her in a high tower in the middle of a huge forest. As years went by her golden hair grew so long and thick that the witch could use it to climb up into the tower.

One day, a prince was riding through the forest when he came across the witch as she arrived to visit Rapunzel. The witch didn't notice the him, and cried out: "Rapunzel! Rapunzel! Let down your hair!" The golden braid came tumbling out of the window and the witch soon climbed up. The prince waited till the witch had left, then called out the same words and climbed up himself.

Rapunzel was enchanted to meet the prince, and they soon fell in love. The prince began to plan Rapunzel's escape, and every day he brought a silken strand, which Rapunzel would weave into a ladder. But one day, Rapunzel forgot herself and told her, "the prince climbs much quicker."

The witch was furious! She grabbed a pair of scissors, cut off Rapunzel's braid, then magicked her to a faraway desert. When the prince arrived later that day the witch let down the braid, but as he neared the top she let go! The prince fell all the way to the ground, landing on some bushes with sharp thorns. He survived, but he was blinded by his fall. The prince then wandered for months — until at last he came to the desert where Rapunzel had been banished.

When Rapunzel saw him she threw her arms around him, crying tears of joy — and as her tears fell onto the prince's eyes, they healed. He could see once more! Finally he led Rapunzel back to his kingdom — where they lived happily ever after.

The Brave Tin Soldier

One Christmas, a little boy was given twenty-five tin soldiers. They were all exactly alike except for one, which only had one leg. There hadn't been enough tin to finish him.

The little boy started playing with his new toys, arranging them by a little cardboard castle. By the castle stood a cardboard lady. She was a dancer and one of her legs was raised so high that the tin soldier thought that she, like himself, had only one leg.

'That is the wife for me,' he thought. He was determined to get to know the dancer somehow.

The little boy lined up the tin soldiers along the windowsill. But alas, the one-legged tin soldier got blown out of the window.

He landed in the street below, and was soon spotted by two boys. They made a paper boat, placed the tin soldier in it, then sent him sailing down the canal. Finally, his boat began to sink, and as the water closed over his head, he thought of the beautiful little dancer whom he would never see again.

But just then the soldier was swallowed up by a fish! How dark it was inside its mouth! He waited… and waited… and finally daylight opened over him. A voice cried out, "I don't believe it, here is the missing tin soldier!" The fish had been caught, taken to the market and sold to the little boy's mother.

Unfortunately, later that day the little boy accidentally dropped the soldier onto the fire — so he never did get to meet the cardboard dancer, and when the boy's mother cleared away the ashes all that remained was his little tin heart.

The Fox without a Tail

Once upon a time, a fox caught his tail in a trap. He struggled and struggled to get free, and in the end he broke loose – but his tail was left behind.

The fox was embarrassed about no longer having a tail but he was determined to put a bold face upon his misfortune, and summoned all the foxes to a meeting.

When everyone had assembled, the fox proposed that all foxes should do away with their tails. He pointed out how inconvenient a tail was when they were pursued by dogs and when they wanted to sit down. "That is all very well," said one of the older foxes, "but I do not think you would have asked us to cut off our tails if you had not lost your own."

Do not trust interested advice.

Mercury and the Woodman

Long ago the god Mercury came to the help of a woodman who had lost his axe in a river. He dived into the water and reappeared – holding a golden axe. The woodman was of course tempted to say it was his – but didn't.

Then Mercury brought up a silver axe.

"No, that's not mine either," said the woodman.

Finally, Mercury recovered the real axe. He was so pleased with the woodman's honesty that he gave him the other axes.

The woodman soon told the story to his friends. One of them was so jealous that he dropped his axe in too. Mercury appeared, and dived and again brought up a golden axe. The man cried, "That's mine!" But Mercury was so disgusted at his dishonesty that he took away the golden axe and left the other one in the river.

Honesty is the best policy.

King Solomon and the Baby

The wise King Solomon used to judge people's arguments and help them solve disputes. One day two women came before him, both claiming that the baby they had brought with them was their own.

"This is my baby – hers died," said one woman.

"No, it's mine," insisted the other.

King Solomon thought for a while then said, "You both say the baby is yours – the simplest thing to do is cut the baby in half and give you half each. Do you agree?"

"Yes," said one woman.

But the other cried out, "No! No! Let her have it. I withdraw my claim."

"Take your baby," said Solomon to the one who had said no. "You are clearly the true mother. You would give it up sooner than let it suffer harm."

The Sphinx

Many years ago in Egypt, there was a monster called the Sphinx. It had a lion's body and a woman's head.

Every time a traveller passed the Sphinx she caught them, and would only let them go if they could answer her question:

"What animal goes on four legs in the morning, two legs at noon, and three legs in the evening?"

No one could answer the question until one day a young man called Oedipus came travelling. The Sphinx asked her riddle and Oedipus answered:

"Man. In childhood he crawls on hands and knees, as a grown-up he walks upright on two legs, but in old age he needs a stick to help him."

At this the Sphinx uttered a cry, sprang from the rock into the valley below, and died. Oedipus had guessed the answer correctly and people no longer travelled in fear.

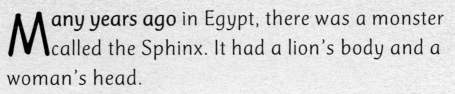

Thumbelina

There was once a woman whose daughter never grew taller than a thumb, so her mother called her Thumbelina.

They lived very happily together until one night, a horrid mother toad thought to herself, 'Thumbelina is the perfect wife for my son.' At the first opportunity the toad grabbed Thumbelina and put her upon a floating water lily leaf in the middle of a stream. Thumbelina began sobbing — she didn't want to marry a toad!

Some fish heard her cries and thought they would help her escape, so they nibbled at the stem until the leaf was swept away.

All summer, Thumbelina lived alone in the woods. She ate honey and drank dew. When winter came and she had to search for shelter, Thumbelina met a field mouse who said, "You can live with me while its cold." So Thumbelina went to live in his burrow.

One day the field mouse's friend, Mr Mole, came to visit. He was charmed by Thumbelina and invited her and the field mouse to come and visit him. So the next day they went through tunnels to Mr Mole's house. On their way they passed a poor dead swallow on the ground. While Thumbelina was at Mr Mole's, she couldn't stop thinking about the poor swallow who should have been out in the open air. So that night she crept back down the tunnel with a blanket to spread over him… and heard a soft *thump, thump*. It was the bird's heart! He was not dead, only numb with cold. Soon the blanket warmed him up.

"Thank you," he gasped.

Thumbelina looked after the swallow in secret all through the winter. Then, when spring arrived, Mr Mole announced he was going to marry her. "You're lucky," the field mouse told her, "he will make a splendid husband." But Thumbelina wept as though her heart would break. She could not bear the thought of living underground, never to be out in the warm sunshine again.

"I am strong enough to leave now," the swallow told her. "Climb on my back and I will take you away with me."

"Oh yes, please!" said Thumbelina.

So up they soared out into the clear bright air. At last they came to a warm country and the swallow put Thumbelina down in the middle of a flower. In the centre of it was the spirit of the flower, who took the form of a tiny prince. They soon fell in love and lived happily ever after.

The Olive Tree and the Fig Tree

High on a hill, there lived an olive tree. It taunted its neighbour, the fig tree, about how she lost her leaves every autumn. "Your leaves fall off each year when the weather turns colder, and you stay bare until the spring. Whereas I, as you see, stay green all year round."

Soon after that the frosts of winter came. The weather was harsh and there was a heavy fall of snow. The snow settled on the tiny leaves of the olive tree like a thick blanket – she was so bowed down with the weight that her branches bent and broke. But the snowflakes fell harmlessly through the bare branches of the fig.

People who boast about their wealth or their fortune can meet with unexpected disaster.

The Chattering Magpie

There was once a woman who had a magpie that could talk, and it told everything that it saw.

Now it happened that the woman's husband had a fine, large eel in a tub. He was planning to serve it to a friend for dinner, but one day while he was away, his wife caught the eel, cooked it, and ate it herself. When her husband came home, her magpie said, "Master, my mistress ate the eel."

As soon as the man left, the woman grabbed the magpie and pulled every last feather from its head. "That's your punishment for telling on me," she said.

From that time on, whenever the magpie saw a bald-headed person, it would squawk, "You too must have told about the eel!"

The Cheese Thief

One afternoon, a man reached into his bag for his lunch and realized that he had been robbed! The chunk of cheese that he had been looking forward to eating had gone!

"Go and search the roads," said his wife, "Look in the alleys and find the man eating your cheese."

But the man had a better idea. "That cheese is so strong and salty," he said, "that whoever has taken it will soon need a drink of water." So instead of bustling about, he seated himself by the village well, and sat there at his ease.

In a short while a stranger came up to take a drink — and when the man searched his pack, there was the cheese!

Puss in Boots

A miller's son inherited a cat from his father. "What am I to do with a cat?" he said. Imagine his surprise when Puss replied, "Give me some boots and a bag and you shall see!"

So the son did as Puss asked. Puss went to a field and put carrots in the bag, then he hid in the grass. Before long, a rabbit hopped into the bag, tempted by the carrots. Off Puss ran to the palace, where he offered the rabbit to the king as a gift from the Marquis of Carabas. The king was delighted.

The next day, Puss said to the miller's son, "Come to the river and help me fish." Puss knew the king would be driving by in his carriage.

"Quick, get into the water!" said Puss. The miller's son did, just as the carriage passed by. Then Puss hid his master's clothes. "STOP!" cried Puss. "My master, the Marquis of Carabas, has been robbed! Thieves stole his clothes as he swam in the river!"

The king gave the miller's son some clothes, then invited him to ride home in his carriage. "It's this way, Your Majesty," said Puss, and he ran on ahead. He met some workers gathering hay in the fields. "When the king's carriage drives by, the king will ask who owns this land," said Puss. "Say it belongs to the Marquis of Carabas." Sure enough, this is what happened. The king was impressed.

Once again, Puss ran ahead. He came to a big castle and asked to meet the ogre that lived there. "What do you want?" the ogre growled.

Puss said, "Is it true you can turn yourself into any animal? Can you turn into a lion?" The ogre did so with ease. "It must be easy to turn into a big animal," said Puss. "Could you turn into a mouse?"

Puss seized his chance – as soon as the ogre changed into a mouse, he pounced and ate him up.

Suddenly, Puss heard the King's carriage arrive. He went outside to meet the king, who was so impressed with the castle that he offered the Marquis of Carabas his daughter's hand in marriage! Puss was very pleased at the way his plan had worked out and spent the rest of his days living in luxury.

The Wind and the Sun

The Wind and the Sun had a dispute as to which was the stronger of the two. "Do you see that traveller?" said the Wind. "Let's try our strength on him. Whoever can strip him of his cloak will be the winner."

"Agreed," said the Sun.

The Wind began first. He blew a blast that made the traveller stagger. But the traveller only drew his cloak tightly around his shoulders, and kept on his way.

Then the Sun tried. He beamed down upon the traveller's head and shoulders. "Ah!" cried the man, "It is so hot!" Then he threw off his cloak, and carried it under his arm.

After that, the Wind never claimed to be stronger than the Sun.

The Bat, the Bramble and the Seagull

A bat, a bramble, and a seagull once decided to go on a voyage together. The bat borrowed some money for the trip, the bramble brought clothes, and the seagull gathered an amount of lead. They loaded a ship and sailed away but they soon hit a great storm. The boat sank but luckily, the three travellers were washed ashore.

Ever since then, the seagull flies over the sea, every now and then diving below the surface, looking for the lead he's lost.

The bat is so afraid of meeting the moneylenders he borrowed from that he only comes out at night. And the bramble catches hold of the clothes of everyone who passes by, hoping someday to recover its lost garments.

People care more about recovering what they have lost than acquiring what they lack.

Nasreddin Hodja and the Smell of Soup

A **starving beggar** passed a restaurant with cauldrons of delicious soup. He was so hungry that he couldn't help but lean over and take a deep breath. At that moment the innkeeper seized him. "You haven't paid!" he exclaimed.

"But I've had nothing," said the beggar. "You must pay for the smell," insisted the innkeeper. The poor beggar had no money to pay, so the innkeeper dragged him off to the judge, Nasreddin Hodja. He listened to the story then said, "I myself will pay you."

Hodja held some coins up to the innkeeper's ear and shook his hand. "Now you may go," he said.

The innkeeper said angrily, "but my payment…"

"This man took the smell of the soup," said Hodja, "and you have been paid with the sound of the money. Now go on your way."

The Red Shoes

Once, there lived a little girl called Karen whose family couldn't afford to buy her shoes. The shoemaker's wife felt sorry for her so she took some leftover red leather and made her some.

Soon after, Karen's mother very sadly died. As Karen walked home from the funeral, a fine carriage passed by. Inside was a rich old lady who felt so sorry for her that she adopted the little girl. Karen was given lovely new clothes and shoes, and people told her she was beautiful.

When the queen and little princess visited their town, the rich old lady took Karen to see them.

Karen saw that the princess had a lovely silk dress and a pair of red leather shoes. They were even prettier than the ones that the shoemaker's wife had made. The next time the old lady took Karen to buy shoes, Karen insisted on choosing a pair of red shoes just like the ones the princess had worn.

The old lady couldn't see well so she didn't realize when Karen wore her bright red shoes to church. All the time she was meant to be saying her prayers, she was admiring her shiny red shoes, which wasn't polite. After the service, several people told the old lady about Karen's shoes. She was extremely cross and said Karen must wear black shoes in future.

But when the next Sunday came around, Karen put on her red shoes again. At the end of the service, an old beggar-man was waiting outside. "What pretty dancing shoes!" he said to Karen. "Never come off when you dance," he told the shoes.

Karen couldn't resist dancing a few steps, but once she began, she couldn't stop! She danced away from the church, down the street and around the corner... and then all the way out of the town. All she could do was dance, over fields and valleys, in the rain and the sun, by day and by night.

She danced for weeks, until she finally danced

right back into the church. There, she begged God to forgive her. All at once, Karen's stopped dancing.

From then on, Karen's feet were so sore that she had to hobble around on crutches, but she never once complained. And no one ever spoke to her again about the red shoes.

The Water of Life

Long ago, a king in a far-off country fell gravely ill. His son was dreadfully upset and feared that his father would die, but one day a little dwarf appeared. "I know something that would save your father," he whispered, "the Water of Life."

He went on, "You will find it in an enchanted castle not too far from here. Here is an iron wand — when you reach the castle, hit the door three times with it and it will open. Throw this bread to the lions and they will not eat you up. Then hurry in and find the well — but be quick, for when the clock strikes twelve, the castle door will shut and you will be trapped there forever."

The prince thanked the dwarf many times and his new friend showed him the road he should take.

When the prince arrived at the castle, everything was as the dwarf had told him.

At the third rap with the wand, the door flew open. He threw the bread and when the lions were eating, he hurried on into the depths of the castle, looking for the well. At last, the prince found it. He drew up the bucket and poured water into a bottle, but just then the clock began to strike…

One! Two! Three! The prince dashed back through the courtyards…

Four! Five! Six! He sped through the castle…

Seven! Eight! Nine! He raced past the lions.

Ten! Eleven! He reached the castle door and leapt through.

Twelve! He heard the heavy door clang shut behind him forever.

He got back on his horse and set off home at a gallop. As soon as he got back he gave his father the Water of Life to drink and the king soon recovered. He arranged a splendid feast to celebrate — and of course the ugly little dwarf was the most important guest.

The Impostor

One day a sick man prayed to the gods to help him, and promised that if he got better, he would sacrifice one hundred oxen to them.

The gods were curious to see how the man would keep this promise. So they made him recover in double-quick time. The man then made one hundred little oxen out of wax and offered them up to the gods. The gods were furious!

The next night the gods sent the man a dream telling him to go to the seashore where he would find one hundred gold coins.

The day after the man hurried to the shore. However once there, a band of robbers captured him and carried him off to sell as a slave. The price he fetched was one hundred gold coins.

Do not promise more than you can deliver.

The Lion, Jupiter and the Elephant

The lion, for all his size and strength, couldn't bear the sound of a cockerel crowing. He was very embarassed about his fear, and didn't like to talk about it. One day the lion met the elephant and the two got talking. While they chatted, the lion couldn't help but notice how often the elephant flapped his ears. Then a tiny gnat came humming by, and the elephant said, "Do you see that little buzzing insect? I'm terribly afraid that it will get into my ear."

The lion's spirits rose at once when he heard this. "For," he said to himself, "if the elephant, huge as he is, is afraid of a gnat, I needn't be so much ashamed of being afraid of a cockerel, which is ten thousand times bigger than a gnat."

There is no shame in being afraid, no matter how big you are.

Buchettino

Once upon a time there was a child whose name was Buchettino. One day he found a penny and bought some figs, and went to eat them in a tree. While he was eating, an ogre passed by, and said, "My dear Buchettino, give me a little fig with your dear little hand. If you don't, I will eat you!"

Buchettino threw him one, but it fell in the dirt. Then the ogre repeated, "My dear Buchettino, please don't throw it — give me a little fig from your dear little hand!"

Poor Buchettino leant down to pass him a fig, and at once the ogre grabbed him and put him in his bag. The ogre set off for home thinking what a delicious meal Buchettino would make.

When the ogre was not far from his house he stopped to rest, and put the bag on the ground. At once Buchettino cut the bag open from within. Then he filled it with large stones, and ran away.

Well, the ogre was furious when he

found out, and he went looking for Bucchetino in the town. At last he saw Buchettino on a balcony, laughing. The ogre nearly burst with rage, but he said, "Buchettino, how did you manage to climb up there?"

Buchettino answered, "I put dishes upon dishes, glasses upon glasses, pans upon pans – afterwards I climbed up on them and here I am."

"Ah! Is that so?" said the stupid ogre. And quickly he made a great mountain of kitchenware. The ogre began to climb up it, but when he was nearly on the top everything fell down and he crashed to the ground. He was so cross that he went off to another country and never troubled Bucchetino again.

The Emperor's New Clothes

Many years ago there lived an emperor who loved new clothes. One day, two men arrived at his court who said they could weave a cloth that only wise people could see, and the emperor immediately ordered an expensive suit from them.

After many days, the weavers announced they were finished and displayed what they said were the clothes. The emperor could see nothing! 'I must be a fool!' he thought. But he dared not admit it. He let the men 'dress' him in the suit and then set out on a parade he had planned to show off his fancy new attire to his subjects. The people could not see the clothes either, but nobody liked to say so. "How magnificent!" they praised.

Suddenly a child's voice called out, "But he's naked!" Everyone realized they'd been tricked. The emperor slunk back to his palace to find the weavers, but they, and all the money he had paid, were long gone.

The Snowdrop

It **was wintertime** and a bulb shot out a little white bud on a stalk, with narrow, thick leaves. Sunbeams shone down to it. "Welcome!" they sang.

The flower was so joyful that she didn't mind when a girl picked her.

One day, the girl wrote a poem about the snowdrop, then posted it in a letter. The letter was opened by the girl's sweetheart who read it delightedly. A while later, however, he became sad. He seized the envelope and threw it away, and the flower drifted to the ground, forgotten.

Next morning a cleaner picked the flower up and thinking it very beautiful, placed it between the pages of a storybook. It stayed there for years until another young man took the book down and began reading. "Why, here's a flower!" he said. "It must have been put here for a special reason! I wonder what its story is..."

The Old Woman in the Wood

Once there was a servant girl who became lost in a dark forest one day. To her surprise, a white dove came flying up to her with a little golden key! It said, "Go to that tree there and use this to open it."

Inside the tree, the girl found bread and milk. Then the white dove gave her a second key. "This key will open that bigger tree," it said. The girl found a beautiful little white bed inside! She had a long sleep and felt refreshed. "Will you do something for me?" asked the little dove.

"Of course," said the girl.

"Thank you," said the dove. "I'll lead you to a small house. Go in without speaking to the witch at the door. You will find yourself in a room filled with rings. Find the plainest one and bring it here."

The girl did as the dove said. She didn't speak a word when the witch opened the door but hurried past her into the room filled with rings. Every surface sparkled with gold and silver and jewels. The girl began hunting for the plain one and finally, tucked away in a corner, she found it.

She took the ring and didn't stop running until she was far away. The girl leant against a tree to rest and suddenly felt the branches behind her move. As they wrapped around her waist they became two arms! The girl turned to find that the tree had become a handsome young man – he kissed her and said, "That old witch cast a spell that made me a dove for two hours every day and a tree for the rest of the time. By taking her enchanted ring you have set me free!"

Then the young man married the brave, kind servant girl and they lived happily ever after.

The Vain Jackdaw

Long ago, the great god Jupiter saw that the birds were arguing among themselves.

He announced that he intended to appoint a king of the birds, to rule over them. The god named a day when he would select the most beautiful bird to be the ruler.

The birds were hugely excited – all of them wished to be chosen. The jackdaw realized that, with his ugly plumage, he would have little chance. So he waited until the others had gone, and then picked up the brightest of the feathers they had dropped, and stuck them all over his body. When the day came, the birds assembled before Jupiter. Just as Jupiter was about to make the jackdaw king, the other birds turned on him and stripped him of his feathers.

Dressing up does not make you a better person.

Fate

King Solomon's servant came breathlessly into the court, "Please! Let me borrow your fastest horse!" he said to the king. "I must be in a town ten miles south of here by nightfall!"

"Why?" asked King Solomon.

"I just met Death in the garden!" said his shuddering servant. "I don't want to be around when he comes to claim me!"

"Very well," said King Solomon. "My fastest horse has hoofs like wings. Take him!" Then the king walked into the garden. He saw Death sitting there, looking confused. "What's wrong?" asked King Solomon.

Death replied, "Tonight I'm supposed to claim the life of the servant I just saw in your garden. But I'm supposed to claim him in a town ten miles south of here! Unless he has a horse with hooves like wings, I don't see how he could get there by nightfall."

November

1 Ten Jugs of Wine

2 St George and the Dragon

3 The Miser and his Gold

4 Everyone is Right

5 Dick Whittington and his Cat

6 The Ants

7 The Heat of a Candle

8 The Seven Ravens

9 The Brother and Sister

10 Robert and the Fairies

11 The Dog, the Rooster and the Fox

12 The Little Horse and its Kind Master

13 The Golden Goose

14 The Rooster and the Pearl

15 The Pied Piper of Hamelin

16 The Silver Coin

17 Belling the Cat

18 A Wild Goose

19 Snow-white and Rose-red

20 The Dancing Gang

21 The Boy Bathing

22 The Farmer and the Boggart

23 The Teapot

24 The Lion and the Statue

25 Nasreddin Hodja's Recipe

26 The Little Red Hen and the Wheat

27 The Spider and the Fly

28 Rumpelstiltskin

29 The Honeybee's Sting

30 How the Moon and Stars Came to Be

Ten Jugs of Wine

It was New Year's Eve, and ten old friends decided to celebrate together with a party. To make it fair they agreed that they would each bring a jug of wine to be poured into a big punch bowl. However, each person thought the same thing: "My wine is too good to share. If I bring water, no one will be able to taste the difference."

And so they gathered together on New Year's Eve and poured the contents of their jugs ceremoniously into the big bowl. Then they ladled out a cup for everyone — and looked guiltily at one another as water was served all round.

St George and the Dragon

St George, the bold knight, once came to a land where a terrible dragon ate a maiden every year. This year it was the turn of the king's daughter, Sabia. The people begged St George for his help, and he agreed to try and save her.

He put on his strongest armour, and with his sword in his hand, rode into the Valley of the Dragon. As soon as the dragon caught sight of the brave knight it spread its burning wings and prepared to attack.

The dragon was so fierce that the knight was nearly knocked to the ground. St George recovered himself and struck a mighty blow with his spear. This made the monster furious! The dragon hit him so violently with its tail that both horse and rider were thrown over.

Purely by chance, St George was flung under the shade of a flowering orange tree, the scent of which had such power that no poisonous beast dare come within its branches — so the dragon could not strike the killing blow! When St George had got his strength back, he rose and struck the burning dragon on his belly. A deadly poison spurted out, burning away his armour but he came forward again, and struck the dragon under one of its flaming wings. The weapon pierced the dragon's heart and all the grass around the dragon turned crimson with blood as the dragon died.

So St George of England cut off the dragon's head and rode on to the king's palace. Sabia washed and bandaged the weary knight's wounds. Then he lay down to rest, while she lulled him to sleep with her golden lute.

The Miser and his Gold

A very greedy man once loved to hoard his money. He grew worried that it might be stolen so he put it in a chest and buried it in his garden.

Every night, the man would dig up the chest, count his coins, then bury his treasure once more. One night, however, a robber saw him dig the chest up. He waited until the man had gone back inside, then dug the chest up himself and stole it. When the greedy man discovered the theft he wailed until his neighbours came. He told them how he used to come and count all his gold.

"Did you ever spend any of it?" asked one neighbour.

"No," said the man.

"Then in future come and look at the hole," said a neighbour, "it will do you just as much good."

If you don't use wealth and treasures, they might as well not exist.

Everyone is Right

Nasreddin Hodja was serving as a judge when a man came to him with a complaint against one of his neighbours.

The Hodja listened to the man carefully then concluded, "Yes, dear neighbour, you are indeed in the right."

Then he called the other man to him and listened to his defence carefully before pronouncing, "Yes, dear neighbour, you are quite right."

The Hodja's wife was sitting beside him, and she turned to him and said, "Husband, the men do not agree with each other so both men cannot be right."

The Hodja simply answered, "Yes, dear wife, you are quite right."

Dick Whittington and his Cat

Hundreds of years ago there lived a poor orphan boy called Dick Whittington. His only possession was a cat. One day they travelled to London and when they arrived, Dick looked around in astonishment. There were so many people and buildings! Before long, he was hopelessly lost. He stumbled into a doorway, and fell fast asleep.

The house belonged to a rich merchant, Mr Fitzwarren. He took Dick and his cat in and gave Dick a job in his kitchen. Dick worked hard, and everyone liked him.

Now, whenever one of Mr Fitzwarren's ships went to sea, he asked everyone in the household to give something to the ship's cargo for luck. Dick had only his cat so he handed her over.

The ship was at sea for many months before it

came to port in China. The crew went ashore to show the emperor the cargo, but to the emperor's embarrassment, the feast that had been prepared for the visitors was ruined by rats.

The captain smiled. "I think I have the answer," he said and he sent for Dick's cat. Within minutes, there were piles of dead rats. The emperor was so pleased that he gave the captain a ship full of gold.

Back in London, Dick had decided to return home but he had not gone far when he heard the church bells ringing. They seemed to say,

"Turn again Whittington,
Thrice Lord Mayor of London."

Dick decided to stay in the city, and when the ships came home, Mr Fitzwarren gave Dick his share of the gold, and more. This was the start of Dick's prosperity. He went on to become Lord Mayor of London three times. He never forgot his early poverty, founding hospitals and schools for the poor. And there were always lots of cats in his house as well!

The Ants

Long ago, ants were people and made their living by farming the land. However, they were always looking longingly at their neighbours' crops, which seemed much better than their own. Whenever they could lay their hands on their neighbours' produce, they stole it, and hid it in their storehouses.

When father of the gods, Jupiter, saw how things had become, he was disgusted with humankind. He was so furious that he changed the bad people into ants! Although their bodies changed, their nature remained the same, so to this day, ants go about the cornfields and gather the fruits of others' labours – and store them up for their own use.

You may punish a thief, but he will always remain a thief.

The Heat of a Candle

Mula bet his friends that he could survive a night on an icy mountain with nothing whatsoever to keep him warm. He set out to win his bet, taking only a book and a candle. Mula shivered all through the night but when he came down, his friends asked, "Did you take anything with you?"

"No," said Mula, "just a book and a small candle to read by."

"What!" they said, "Then you had some heat – you lose!"

A week later Mula invited his friends to dinner. They waited for hours for the food to be ready. "Dinner is taking a long time," said Mula, "Come and see why!"

In the kitchen there was a huge pot of water under which a small candle was burning. Mula said, "I've been trying to heat this pot of water over this candle since yesterday and it's not warm yet!"

The Seven Ravens

There was once a widow who had seven sons and one daughter. The daughter was sweet and good-natured, but the boys were loud and wild. One day, when they were causing trouble, the widow cried, "I wish you would all turn into ravens!" The next second, her sons had vanished and seven black birds flew out of the window and away.

Their little sister was so upset that she decided to set out into the wide world to find her brothers, taking nothing with her but a little ring.

She journeyed till she came to the sun, but it looked much too hot and fiery. She then ran away quickly to the moon, but the moon was cold and chilly, so she travelled on and came to the stars, and they were friendly and kind to her. The morning star gave her a little bone, and said, "With this you can unlock the glass-mountain, and there your brothers live."

The little girl went on until she came to the glass-mountain, and found the door shut. She felt for the bone but found she had lost it! Desperate to save her brothers she took a knife from her pocket and after many hours of work she managed to pick the lock.

Inside she found a table set with seven little plates and glasses. She took a drink from each glass and let the ring fall into the last one.

Suddenly she heard a fluttering and croaking in the air, and she hid behind the door. Seven ravens appeared and looked for their little plates and glasses. Then said one after the other, "Who has eaten from my little plate? And who has been drinking out of my little glass?"

When the seventh came to the bottom of his glass, he said, "Has our little sister come? If so we shall be free!" When the little girl heard this, she ran forward, and in an instant all her brothers took their true form again. They hugged and kissed each other, and went merrily home.

The Brother and Sister

Once upon a time, there lived a couple who had two children, a boy and a girl. The boy was very good-looking, but the girl was very plain. To save conflict, the children's parents made sure that they never saw their reflections.

However one day, they went to play in their mother's chamber, and found her mirror. The boy saw how handsome he was, and began to boast to his sister, but she was ready to cry at her plainness. She ran to her father to moan about her brother's vanity. The man just laughed, and said, "Now you have seen yourselves, make good use of the mirror. My boy, try to be as kind as you are handsome, and you, my girl, resolve to develop the sweetness of your nature."

Good qualities are more important than beauty.

Robert and the Fairies

Robert Roberts was a carpenter who worked very hard indeed. One day, a little man came up to him and said: "Robert Roberts, go to the holly tree on the hill, dig below it, and you'll be rewarded."

Next morning, Robert Roberts did as he was told and he found a box of gold. He returned every week, and found gold each time! But as he grew rich, he began to boast about his mysterious friends.

One day he told someone who he wanted to impress that he was friends with the fairies. A week later, he went back for more gold, as usual, but when he reached the tree big stones came rolling down the bank! Robert Roberts had to run for his life, and he never went near the place again. Fairies don't like people who tell about them.

The Dog, the Rooster and the Fox

A dog and a rooster became great friends, and agreed to go on a journey together. They travelled all day, and at dusk found a tree that looked like a good place to sleep. The rooster flew up into the branches, and the dog curled up inside the hollow tree trunk.

At dawn the rooster awoke and began to crow. Hearing this, a hungry fox came and stood under the tree and begged him to come down. "I should like," said the fox, "to get to know one who has such a beautiful voice."

The rooster wasn't fooled. He replied, "Would you wake my butler who sleeps at the foot of the tree? He'll let you in." So the fox rapped on the trunk, out rushed the dog – and that was the end of the fox!

Do not be taken in by flattery.

The Little Horse and its Kind Master

There **was once** a foolish man of Gotham who
started for market with a heavy sack of wheat
laid across his horse's back, while he sat behind it.
He had not gone far when another man said,
"That's a heavy load. Why do you not walk and lead
your horse?"

"I can't," replied the first man, "My foot is lame."

"Then if you must ride," said the other,
"You should take the bag of wheat
on your shoulder so the horse won't
have to carry that, too."

"All right," said the
first man, and he
hoisted the bag of
wheat to his shoulder.

"Ah," said he, when
he got to market, "My
horse looks exhausted. How
lucky I was able to help him
with the wheat."

The Golden Goose

Once upon a time there was a man who had a son called Duffer. Everyone thought he was a fool and laughed at him.

One day, Duffer went into the forest to chop wood. He was hacking away at a tree when a little man came up and asked him for food and drink. Duffer shared his food and when they had finished the little man said, "Chop down that tree over there and you will find something precious." To his great surprise, Duffer found a goose with feathers made of pure gold sitting in the roots. He picked her up carefully and went off to an inn for the night.

That night, the innkeeper's daughter crept into Duffer's room to look at the goose. She tiptoed over to it and stroked the wing. But her hand got stuck! No matter how much she pulled, she couldn't let go.

Not long afterwards, her sister came creeping in. She too reached out to stroke the golden goose and got stuck! Then a third sister came and the same thing happened to her.

In the morning Duffer picked up the bird and strolled out with the three girls hanging onto it. Soon, they met a vicar who grabbed the youngest girl's hand to pull her away. But as soon as he touched her, he was stuck too! Before long a farmer came by. He touched the vicar's sleeve – and that was that!

"Hey!" called the farmer to two farm-workers. "Come and help me!" But soon they were firmly attached as well! Now there were seven people running behind Duffer and the goose.

Soon they came to a city where there was a princess who never laughed. The king had announced that whoever could make her laugh could marry her. The minute the princess saw Duffer and his golden goose, with all the people stuck fast behind them, she burst out laughing!

The king was delighted and the royal wedding took place at once, with much celebrating and rejoicing.

The Rooster and the Pearl

A proud rooster was strutting up and down the farmyard among the hens one morning when he suddenly spied something shining in the straw. "Ho! Ho!" said the rooster. "Whatever it is, it's for me."

He looked all around to check that no one was watching him, then he scratched and pecked, and rooted the object out from beneath the straw. It turned out to be a pearl that had somehow been lost in the yard.

Although it was clearly very beautiful, the rooster was mightily disappointed. "To humans, you may be a treasure," he sighed. "But I would much rather have a single barley seed to eat than a whole string of pearls, for they are of no use to me."

Precious things are for those that can prize them.

The Pied Piper of Hamelin

The town of Hamelin had become plagued with rats and its people were in utter despair. They had almost lost hope when one day, a strange man appeared. He promised to rid the town of the pests for a fee, and the town council agreed. So he put a pipe to his lips and when he played all the rats followed him. He led them to the river where they all drowned.

But when the piper asked for his money, the council refused. With a grim smile, the piper put the pipe to his lips again, and this time all the children followed wherever he piped – all except one who was lame. He led them far away and the townspeople never saw the children again.

The Silver Coin

Lots of coins were being made at a mint when a silver coin came out very excited, shouting, "Hooray! Now I am going out into the wide world."

And so it did. The coin was used by many people to pay for things before he came to a man who was about to travel to many different countries. The traveller decided to keep the silver coin with him for good luck.

But one day, the coin slipped out of the man's pocket! It was soon found by a woman, but when she tried to use it to pay for something, the shopkeeper pointed out to her that it was from a different country, and he wouldn't accept it.

The poor silver coin realized that, so far from home, it couldn't be used as money at all! The woman kept it anyway but a man stole it from her and then sneaked it in with some other coins to buy a lottery ticket. The silver coin never found out whether the lottery ticket had won – it hoped that it hadn't!

The coin continued to be passed from person to person – always slipped in with other coins to make it less noticeable – until one day it was passed back to the same traveller who had brought it from home. A smile spread over his face and he said, "A coin from my own country. How strange that it's somehow come into my hands. It must be lucky!"

At last, the traveller returned home – and the silver coin finally felt safe once more. From then on, it told everyone it met that when times get tough, you should never give up hope – for if you stay strong and behave honestly, everything will turn out all right in the end.

Belling the Cat

Long ago, a group of mice were terrorized by a cat.

The mice held a meeting to discuss how they could outwit their enemy. Some said this, and some said that, but at last a young mouse got up and said, "You will all agree that our danger lies in the sly way in which the enemy lurks about, waiting for us. If we could receive some signal of her approach, we could easily escape. I therefore propose that we get a small bell and attach it round the neck of the cat. Then we will always know where she is and when she is coming."

This proposal met with a lot of clapping, until an old mouse got up and said, "But who is going to volunteer to tie the bell on the cat?"

It is easy to think up impossible solutions.

A Wild Goose

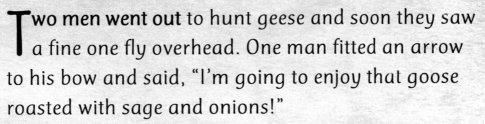

Two men went out to hunt geese and soon they saw a fine one fly overhead. One man fitted an arrow to his bow and said, "I'm going to enjoy that goose roasted with sage and onions!"

"Sage and onions!" exclaimed the other, "NO! Apple sauce and green peas is the only way to cook goose."

"Sage!" insisted the other.

"Apple!"

"Sage!"

"Apple!"

"Right," said the man, "Let's ask our village headman."

The village headman was very wise and declared the goose should be cooked half one way and half the other. The men were content with this and went back to fire the arrow... but of course the goose was long gone.

Snow-white and Rose-red

A **poor widow** lived with her two daughters, Snow-white and Rose-red. The girls did everything together and promised never to leave each other.

One freezing winter's night there was a knock at the door. It was a big, black bear! The bear said gently, "Please don't be frightened — all I want is to warm up in front of your fire."

Snow-white and Rose-red took pity on the bear and let him in. He was very well behaved, and soon they were quite comfortable with him. They even brushed the snow from his shaggy fur.

The next night the bear arrived at the same time in the evening, and again spent the night by the fire. And so it went all winter, with the bear knocking at their door at the same time each evening.

Then one day, spring arrived. That morning, the bear said, "Now I must go away."

"But where will you go, dear bear?" asked Snow-white.

"Into the forest, to guard it from wicked dwarfs." The girls were very sad, but the bear promised to return next winter.

One week later, the sisters went into the forest to fetch firewood. Near a fallen tree, they saw an angry dwarf, who had got the end of his long beard caught in the tree trunk. Snow-white cut off the end of the beard, freeing him.

"You stupid girl! You've cut off a piece of my beard!" the dwarf cried, most ungratefully.

Soon afterwards, the girl's mother sent them to town to buy needles. On the way they saw an eagle seize the very same dwarf and attempt to carry him off. The girls grabbed hold of the little man and pulled against the eagle so hard that at last it let go and flew off.

"You've ripped my coat to pieces!" the dwarf yelled. "I'll curse you!" Just as he began to mutter a wicked spell, there was a loud growl and a huge bear came galloping out of the forest. He killed the dwarf with one swipe of his paw.

The girls stood trembling. But the bear said, "Do not be afraid." And at once they recognized their friend. As it walked towards them the bear transformed into a handsome man, dressed in gold. "I am a king's son," he said, "and I was bewitched by that dwarf. At long last he is dead and the spell is broken."

Everyone was full of joy. Snow-white married the prince and Rose-red married his brother. And they all lived happily together for many years.

The Dancing Gang

A water carrier on a building site once went to the river to fetch some water. She dipped in her pot, and found she had caught a crayfish. The crayfish began beating his claws on the pot, and played such a beautiful tune that the girl began dancing, and could not stop.

The leader of the building site wondered why she had not come back, and sent another girl to look for her. When she found her, she too began to dance. Then the driver sent another and another, till he had sent the whole gang of workers.

At last he went himself and when he found the whole gang dancing, he too began to dance — and they all danced till night! They didn't stop even when the crayfish went back into the water, and if they haven't stopped dancing, they are dancing still.

The Boy Bathing

A boy once fancied bathing in the river, as it was a hot day and the water looked so fresh and cool. He wasn't a very good swimmer, but he stripped off his clothes and stepped into the water.

He began jumping about and splashing — until suddenly the river bed dropped away from him and his feet could no longer touch the ground. He was right out of his depth and in danger of drowning.

Fortunately, a man who was passing heard his cries for help. He went to the riverside and began to scold him for being so careless as to get into deep water. "Oh, sir," cried the boy, "please help me first and tell me off afterwards."

Give assistance, not advice, in a crisis.

The Farmer and the Boggart

Once upon a time a man grew some wheat in a field. As he was preparing to reap it, a boggart burst out of the earth and told him to be gone. "'Tis my land here," he shrieked. "Mine, mine!"

The farmer thought to himself, then suggested that whoever could reap the most wheat should get the field. The boggart agreed and the next day they both started collecting the crop. The farmer had been crafty, however, and had placed iron rods on the boggart's side of the field. The farmer cut more and more wheat and at last the boggart threw down its scythe. "This wheat is impossible to cut! You may take the land!" it cried.

So the farmer lived happily ever after — and the boggart was never seen again.

The Teapot

Once there was a very proud teapot made of fine china. She would talk to anyone who would listen about her long spout and graceful handle. She boasted about her delicate, beautiful design all the time and would never let anyone forget it.

"Without me, everyone would go thirsty! The people could drink their tea out of glasses or bowls, so the teacups aren't of that much value. But without me — why, no one could drink tea at all!"

Now the cream jug, the sugar bowl and the teacups and saucers were very tired of hearing the teapot talk in this way — especially when they knew her lid was cracked and chipped!

"Who does she think she is?" the cream jug protested.

As the teapot talked on and on, they all sighed to each other. Then one day, the person pouring out the tea dropped the teapot! She fell to the floor, her spout broke in half and her handle snapped off. Once the other members of the tea set had got over the shock, they couldn't help but burst out laughing!

The people cleared the mess away. "Glue won't fix this, but we could use it as a plant pot instead," suggested somebody.

So that's what they did. They filled the teapot with earth and then planted a flower bulb in it. The teapot was pleased, for now she had a heart. "I have never had a living heart until now," she said to herself. "I must be even more important than ever."

So the teapot was very happy sitting on the kitchen windowsill, with thoughts and feelings and a pretty red flower to love.

And the cream jug, sugar bowl and cups and saucers welcomed a brand new teapot on to the tea table, who was modest and polite and fitted into the tea set very well.

The Lion and the Statue

Once upon a time, a man and a lion were travelling companions on a long journey. In the course of conversation they began to boast about how strong and bold they were, each claiming to be more courageous than the other.

And so they went on, squabbling all the way, until they came to a crossroads where there was a statue of a man overpowering a lion.

"There!" said the man triumphantly. "Look at that. Doesn't that prove that men are stronger than lions?"

"Not so fast, my friend," said the lion, "that is only your view of the contest. If lions could make statues, you may be sure that you would see the man underneath."

There are two sides to every story.

Nasreddin Hodja's Recipe

Nasreddin Hodja bought a piece of meat at the market, and on his way home he met a friend. Seeing the meat in Nasreddin's hand, the friend told him an excellent recipe for stew.

"I'll forget it for sure," said Nasreddin. "Write it on a piece of paper for me."

The friend wrote it down, and Nasreddin continued on his way, the piece of meat in one hand and the recipe in the other. He had not walked far when suddenly a large hawk swooped down from the sky, snatched the meat, and flew away with it.

"It won't do you any good!" shouted Nasreddin after the disappearing hawk. "I still have the recipe!"

The Little Red Hen and the Wheat

One day a little red hen found a grain of wheat in the barnyard, and said, "Who will plant this wheat?"

"I won't," said the dog.

"I won't," said the cat.

"I won't," said the goose.

"I won't," said the turkey.

"I will, then," said the little red hen. "Ca-ca-ca-ca-ca-ca-ca-ca-daa-cut!"

So she planted the grain of wheat. The sun shone and the rain fell and the wheat grew until it had a big head of ripe grain at the top.

"Who will reap this wheat?" said the little red hen.

"I won't," said the dog, the cat, the goose, and the turkey.

"I will, then," said the little red hen. "Ca-ca-ca-ca-ca-ca-ca-ca-daa-cut!"

So she reaped the wheat. Then she said, "Who will thresh this wheat?"

"I won't," chorused the dog, the cat, the goose, and the turkey.

"I will, then," said the little red hen. "Ca-ca-ca-ca-ca-ca-ca-ca-daa-cut!"

So she threshed the wheat. "Who will take this wheat to the mill to have it ground?" said the little red hen.

"I won't," called the dog, the cat, the goose, and the turkey.

"I will, then," said the little red hen. "Ca-ca-ca-ca-ca-ca-ca-ca-daa-cut!"

So she took the wheat to the mill, and by and by she came back with the flour.

"Who will bake this flour?" said the little red hen.

"I won't," replied the dog, the cat, the goose, and the turkey.

"I will, then," said the little red hen. "Ca-ca-ca-ca-ca-ca-ca-ca-daa-cut!"

So she baked the flour and made a loaf of bread.

"Who will eat this bread?" said the little red hen.

"I will," said the dog.

"I will," said the cat.

"I will," said the goose.

"I will," said the turkey.

"I will," said the little red hen. "Ca-ca-ca-ca-ca-ca-ca-ca-daa-cut!" and she ate the loaf of bread all up.

The Spider and the Fly

Mr Spider wanted to marry Miss Fly. Many times he told her of his love and begged her to become his wife, but she always refused, for she did not like him.

One day when she saw Mr Spider coming, Miss Fly closed all the doors and windows of her house and got a pot of boiling water. Then she waited, and when Mr Spider called, begging her to allow him to enter, she answered by throwing boiling water at him. This made Mr Spider very angry and he cried, "I will never forgive you for this! My descendants and I will always despise you – we will never give you any peace."

Mr Spider kept his word, and even today you can see how much spiders hate flies.

Rumpelstiltskin

One day a miller told a lie to make his family seem more important. "My daughter knows how to spin straw into gold!" he boasted.

The news spread to the king and he ordered the girl to be brought to his palace. To her horror, the king showed her to a room piled with straw and ordered her to spin it into gold by morning. Then he locked her in.

But as the girl started to cry, a little man appeared and said he would help her if she would give him her first-born child. The miller's daughter was so desperate that she agreed. The little man sat down and span bundle after bundle of straw into gold.

The next morning the king could not believe his eyes.

He was so impressed that he decided to marry the miller's daughter the very next day.

They were very happy together, and a year later she gave birth to a son. Her happiness was complete – until the little man suddenly appeared. "Give me what you promised," he demanded.

The queen offered him everything else she had but he refused. At last he agreed that if she could guess his name he would let her off. He would give her three days to find it out. Then he vanished. The queen thought frantically of every name she had ever heard and sent out messengers to search for other names, but two days went by and she knew in her heart that they had not yet found the right one.

Late on the last evening a messenger returned and said, "Many miles from here I came across a little man dancing in the woods. He was singing, 'No one can guess that Rumpelstiltskin is my name!'"

When the little man appeared that night to claim the child the queen said to him, "Is there any chance that you could be called... Rumpelstiltskin?"

"WHO TOLD YOU?" roared the little man. He jumped up and down so hard that the ground beneath his feet split open and swallowed him up – and he was never ever seen again.

The Honeybee's Sting

Zeus, the king of Mount Olympus, said he would give each animal, bird or insect a gift to help them through their life. Some chose to be able to run fast, some to have thick scales to protect them, some to have stripes or patterns to disguise them. To Zeus' surprise, the little honeybee came before his throne and said, "For my gift, I'd like the power to inflict great pain whenever I choose."

"What a cruel wish!" said great Zeus, "I will grant it because I promised I would. But you will have to choose when you use this gift very carefully because using it will cost you your life."

And to this day, the little honeybee dies after it stings.

How the Moon and Stars Came to Be

One day in the times when the sky was close to the ground a young girl went out to pound rice. Before she began her work, she took off the beads from around her neck and the curved comb from her hair, and hung them on the sky, which at that time hung low all around her like blue coral.

Then she began working, and each time she raised her pestle into the air it hit the sky. For some time she pounded the rice, and then she raised the pestle so high that it struck the sky very hard.

Immediately the sky shot up, and it went up so far that she lost her beads and comb. They never did come down — the curved comb became the moon and the beads are now the stars that are scattered about.

DECEMBER

The Wolf and the Kid

Goats are very good at scrambling up and down steep mountainsides and can often climb where others can't go.

Once upon a time, a young goat clambered on top of a shed in a farmyard and perched on the roof, looking down proudly on everyone below. Just then, a wolf slunk by, casting his eyes around greedily for a meal. Immediately, the kid began to tease the wolf – for he felt quite safe up on the roof.

"Mr Wolf," he cried. "You are a murderer and a thief. I don't know how you dare show your face near the homes of honest folk. We know the crimes you commit!"

"Curse away, my young friend," said the wolf. "You are only being so bold because you know that I can't get my claws into you at the moment."

It is easy to be brave when you are a safe distance from danger.

The Poor Man
and the Angel

A poor woodcutter called Hans once met an old woman who begged him for some food. All Hans had with him was a a tiny amount of vegetable stew in a tin bowl. It was his one daily meal, but he kindly gave it to the stranger. The old woman ate it hungrily then suddenly turned into a radiant angel. She told Hans that because of his kindness, he should never be in want again so long as he lived.

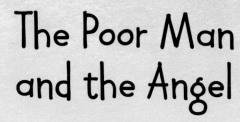

The angel vanished, but from that time forth, everything went well for Hans and he lived in comfort for many years. To remind him of his days of poverty, and to keep himself from becoming proud, he always ate his meals out of his tin bowl.

The Inchcape Rock

In the depths of the North Sea lies the Inchcape Rock. It has wrecked many ships and is a danger to those who roam the water.

To warn sailors of the dangers nearby, the holy Abbot of Aberbrothock put a bell on a buoy next to the rock, and many lives were thankfully saved. However, a wicked sailor called Ralph the Rover hated the Abbot, and to spite him he sank the bell. How could he have guessed that soon he would be in need of the bell himself?

One misty day a few weeks later Ralph's own boat was hit by the Inchcape Rock, and sank with Ralph onboard. We'll never know if he could hear the Abbot's bell, ringing at the bottom of the sea.

The Thistle's Tale

Long ago and far away, a rich family once lived in a large manor house. It had a beautiful garden, filled with beautiful flowers and trees.

There came a time when the family of the house had many visitors from abroad. For two days they entertained their guests in the garden. Someone suggested that the girls should find their favourite flower, so that one of the men could pick it for them.

One pretty girl from Scotland, however, couldn't find a flower she liked until she neared the fence by the roadside. There she saw a large thistle – the flower of Scotland, and she asked the son of the house to pick it for her. After he handed it to her she threaded it carefully through his buttonhole.

The young man was delighted – and so was the thistle bush. "I must be something very special!" it said, "I suppose I should really be inside the garden, not outside the fence. Well, I've managed to get one of my lovely flowers inside at least!"

A few days went by and then a little bird told the thistle bush that the lovely Scottish girl had agreed to marry the son of the house. "And all because of me!" exclaimed the thistle bush. "Now surely someone will dig me up, take me into the garden and replant me there."

But nothing like that happened – the thistle bush remained where it had always been. The summer and autumn went by. Finally, a thought struck the thistle and it announced, "Maybe if you are a parent, and good things happen to your children, you don't mind if good things don't happen to you."

"That's an honourable thought," replied a sunbeam. "And for that, you deserve a good place."

"In a buttonhole, in a pot, or in the house?" asked the thistle.

"In a story, of course!" said the sunbeam.

The Fir Tree and the Bramble

There was once a forest in which there lived a very proud fir tree. She thought she was better than all the other trees because she grew taller and straighter than any other plants around her.

One day she boasted to a bramble in a very snooty manner. She said, "You poor thing, you are of no use whatsoever. Now, look at me — I am useful for lots of things. For instance, when people build houses, they always choose fir. They can't do without me."

The bramble wasn't upset. She replied, "Ah, that's all very well, but you wait until people come with axes to cut you down. Then you'll wish you were a bramble and not a fir."

It is sometimes better to be poor without any cares, than to be rich and weighed down with duties.

Where are the Kittens?

The children came in with their mother from the garden and found the cat sitting in her basket, mewing sadly. Where were her kittens?

"Oh, Mummy," said Alice, "Something is wrong! Look, there's things all over the floor and the kittens are missing. Do you think a fox might have got in and carried them off?"

"I do hope not," said Mummy, looking worried. "It does look as if something big has been in here and messed around — look at that basket on the floor, and all those papers."

They started to tidy up when suddenly Mark gave a shout. He had picked up the basket and there, underneath it, were the three kittens.

"I found the kittens," said Mark, "and I think I found who made the mess too."

The Three Sillies

One evening, a gentleman went to visit the girl he was courting at her parents' home. Soon after he arrived the girl went to the cellar to fetch the beer, and as she looked up she saw an axe stuck in a beam. She said to herself, "Suppose we were to be married, and have a son, and he grew up, came down here and the axe fell on his head and killed him! What a dreadful thing that would be!" And she sat down and cried. After a while her mother went to see why she was taking so long, and she found the beer pouring all over the floor!

"What is the matter?" said her mother.

The girl told her mother what she'd been thinking, and they both sat down to cry together. Then the father began to wonder why they hadn't returned, so he went down to the cellar. "Whatever's the matter?" he said.

"Why," said the mother, "look at that axe." And she told the tale. "Dear, dear!" said the father, and he sat down, and started crying.

Soon the gentleman grew tired of waiting by himself, and he went down to see what they were doing — and there the three sat crying, the beer all over the floor around them. He asked them what they were doing.

"Oh!" said the father, and as he explained their fear they all started crying worse than before. The gentleman burst out laughing. He said, "I've never met such sillies as you three," and he reached up and pulled out the axe.

The Robe of Nasreddin Hodja

Nasreddin Hodja, bruised and limping, met one of his neighbours at the marketplace.

"My dear friend, what has happened to you?" asked the neighbour.

The Hodja answered, "Last night my wife grew angry and kicked my robe down the stairs."

"But how could that have caused your injuries?" asked the neighbour, confused.

"I was wearing the robe at the time," explained Nasreddin, with a frown.

The King and the Puzzle

One day King Solomon was sitting on his throne when the Queen of Sheba walked up to him.

"O King," she said, "Men have told me of your great intelligence. I have here a puzzle that I think will test your wisdom."

Then she held up a beautiful bunch of flowers in each hand.

"One of these bunches," said the queen, "is made of flowers from your garden. The other is made of artificial flowers. Now, tell me, O King, without touching, which is which?"

The king, for once, was puzzled. He frowned. Then he said, "Open the window!"

The next moment a bee entered and flew to the flowers in the queen's right hand.

"O Queen, the bees have given you my answer," said Solomon.

And the queen said, "King Solomon you are very wise — you gather knowledge from the little things."

The Lion's Share

A lion once went hunting with a fox, a jackal and a wolf. Working together, they killed a stag – then discussed how they would share it out.

The lion demanded that they divide it into quarters. "The first quarter is for me," he declared, "because I am King of the Beasts. The second quarter is mine, because I'm sorting out the shares. The third share is mine because I helped hunt the stag. As for the fourth quarter, well, I'd like to see which of you will dare to lay a paw upon it!" And the lion bared his teeth and flexed his claws furiously.

The three other hunters realized they had little hope, and slunk away into the shadows.

Powerful people are more than happy to let you do some of their work, but they won't share the rewards.

The Horse of Brass

Cambuscan was the noblest king in the East. One day, a knight arrived at his palace riding a marvellous brass horse.

"The king of India," the knight said, "has sent you this horse. It can take you anywhere in the world."

The king was very pleased. "Tell me," he said, "how to work it."

"To ride, remove this peg and name the place you wish to go. To stop, turn this wooden pin. If you turn this iron pin, he will vanish, but he'll come back when you call his name."

The knight left, and the king approached the horse. He turned the iron pin and the horse vanished. Only then did King Cambuscan remember the knight had not told him the horse's name!

If you ever go to the palace and shout the name of the brass horse, I'm sure he'll appear.

The Fox and the Little Red Hen

Once upon a time there was a little red hen. She lived near to a fox and his mother.

One day the fox said, "Mother, get a pot boiling, I'm going to go and catch the little red hen."

The fox sneaked into the hen's house and hid behind the door. When the little red hen came in and saw the fox, she was so frightened that she flew up to a peg on the wall.

"Ha, ha!" laughed the fox, "I'll soon get you down," and he began running round and round after his tail.

The little red hen watched him, and soon she got so dizzy she fell off! The fox put her in his bag, and started for home, but he soon grew tired and sat down to rest. Then the little red hen tore a hole in the bag, and jumped out without the fox realizing. She picked up several large stones and put them in the bag in her place, and ran off home.

After a while the fox got up and carried on his journey. "How heavy this little hen is!" he said to himself. "She must be very plump and fat."

When the fox arrived home he called out to his mother, "Have you got the pot boiling?"

"Yes, yes," she replied, "and have you got the little red hen?"

"She's here in this bag," was his answer. "When I count to three, you take the lid off the pot and I'll pop the little red hen into the water."

His mother took the lid off, and as the fox emptied his bag, the stones tumbled into the boiling water, tipping the pot over. The foxes fled as the boiling water splashed out, and never again did they try to catch the little red hen.

The Precious Stove

Poor Peter lived in a rundown old house with only one precious possession — a beautiful gold and white stove that his grandfather had rescued from a burnt-out palace. But one day Peter's father sadly announced, "I've had to sell the stove to buy bread."

When men arrived with a cart to take the stove away, Peter decided to hide inside it and see if he could rescue it. He travelled a long way, and when they stopped moving he poked his head out of the top. Who should he find looking at him but the king!

When he heard Peter's story, he said, "I can't return the stove, for it belongs in our palace, but I will give you a job looking after it, and I will send money to your parents." You can imagine how happy that made Peter!

The Crab and the Fox

There was once a crab who lived in a rock pool at the seashore. He was happy for a time, but soon grew bored and restless, seeing the same surroundings all the time. The crab wanted a change of scenery, so he left the beach and went inland, scurrying sideways.

There, he found a meadow, which he thought looked beautiful – lush and green, and filled with flowers. He settled there, hoping it would be a good place to live. But soon, along came a hungry fox and caught the the crab. The fox had never seen a crab before, and thought he smelled delicious! Just as he was going to be eaten up, the crab said, "This is what I deserve, for I had no business leaving my natural home by the sea and settling here, as though I belonged to the land."

Be content with your lot.

The Pot that would not Walk

One day a man who was known for being silly was getting ready to go to the market. "Husband, we need a new iron pot for the fireplace," said the man's wife.

So the man did his shopping and bought a pot. He placed it on his shoulders and started for home, but it was very heavy. He soon grew tired and set it down.

While he was resting, he noticed that the pot had three legs. "What a pity I didn't see those legs before!" cried the man. "You have three legs and I have only two, and yet I have been carrying you. That doesn't seem fair. Well, you shall take me the rest of the way, at least."

So the man climbed

into the pot and said, "Go on — I am ready." But the pot stood still on its three legs and wouldn't move.

"Ah!" said the man, "you are stubborn, are you? You want me to keep on carrying you, I suppose, but I shan't. I'll tell you the way, and you can stay where you are until you are ready to follow me."

So he told the pot where he lived and how to get there, and off the man went. When he reached home his wife asked him where the pot was.

"Oh, it will be along soon," he replied.

"And what do you mean by that?" she said.

The man explained, but his wife was much more sensible than he was and hurried off to get the pot. When she brought it home the man said, "I am glad you have it safe, wife, for I have been thinking while you were gone that the pot might have decided to walk back to the market if we had left it alone for much longer."

The Spartan's Answer

The people of Sparta, in Greece, were famous for their simple way of life, their skill in battle and their habit of never saying more than they needed to. Near them was a land called Macedon, and this land was at one time ruled over by a war-like king named Philip, who wanted to rule all of Greece.

Philip raised a great army, and made war upon nearby states, until nearly all of them were forced to call him king. Finally, he sent a letter to the Spartans in Laconia, and said, "Surrender now, for if I enter your country, I will level your great cities to the ground."

In a few days, an answer was brought back to Philip. When he opened the letter, he found only one word written there.

That word was "IF."

The Fox and the Crow

A **hungry crow** once spied a piece of cheese on the ground, so she picked it up in her beak and flew into a tree to eat it.

A fox was lurking in some bushes nearby. He spotted the crow and licked his lips at the thought of the cheese. The fox strolled up to the foot of the tree and cried, "Mistress Crow, how well you look today, how glossy your feathers. I'm sure your voice must be just as beautiful. Sing for me, please, so I can tell everyone that you are the Queen of Birds."

The crow was thrilled by this praise. She lifted her head and began to caw — and straightaway the cheese fell to the ground, just as the fox had planned! He pounced on it at once and ate it all up!

Don't trust flatterers.

The Birds in the Wheat Field

The men of Gotham once hired a man to scare the birds away from their wheat field. Unfortunately, the man they asked had very big feet and a lot of the grain was trampled anyway!

"This will never do," said the men, and they tried to come up with a plan. At last one of them said, "We must carry him through the field so that he doesn't squash all the wheat."

"Yes, yes," cried the others, "that's a great idea – why didn't we think of that before?"

So eight men got an old gate, had the man sit on it, and they carried him through the wheat fields as he scared the birds away. "He will not trample any more of our grain with his big feet now," said the silly men of Gotham.

The Lion and the Mouse

Once, a tiny little mouse was caught by a big, hungry lion. "Please let me go, King," cried the mouse, trembling in terror, "and I shall never forget you. I may even be able to help you one of these days." The lion was amused at the thought of the mouse being able to help him, so he let him go.

Sometime after, the lion was caught in a trap. The hunters bound the lion and tethered him to a tree while they went to get a wagon to carry him away. Just then, the little mouse happened to pass by, and he recognized the lion at once. It took the mouse only a few moments before he had gnawed away the ropes and the lion was free.

"You see?" said the little mouse. "Was I not right after all?"

Little friends may prove great friends.

Who was the Luckiest?

Once upon a time, a rose bush stood blooming beautifully in a garden. "What lovely red roses!" laughed the sunshine. "They are all my children, for I kissed them to life."

"No," whispered the dew. "They are my children — for I gave them my tears to drink."

"I am their mother," said the rose bush firmly. "But you are a very special aunt."

At that moment, a woman whose elderly mother had recently passed away, came into the garden. She picked a rosebud and took it to place on her grave. The rosebud trembled with joy. "Surely I am the luckiest flower."

Soon, another woman came walking into the garden. She took the largest rose, and put it in a bowl to make sweet-smelling potpourri.

"What a wonderful honour," sighed the rose. "I am the luckiest, surely."

Then, two young men came strolling along. One was a painter and the other was a poet. Each of them picked a lovely rose. The painter created a picture of his flower.

"This rose will live on, while all the others fade and die," said the painter.

The poet decided to write a poem about his rose, and said, "A painting will fade one day, but a poem can live in people's minds forever."

So every rose had its own story. And every rose was sure that it was the luckiest one.

"I am very lucky too," said the wind, "I know the story of all the roses and I can spread it throughout the world. Perhaps it is I who am the luckiest of all."

So tell me, what do you think?

The Smuggler

A clever smuggler, with a donkey carrying a heavy load of straw, came to a border between two countries. The official at the border was suspicious — he thought the man may have something valuable concealed in the straw. He searched and searched, but found nothing. "I'm certain you're smuggling something," the official said, as the man crossed through. Each day for ten years the same man came to the border with a donkey. Although the official checked the straw bundles everytime, he could never find anything.

Many years later, after the official had retired, he happened to meet that same smuggler in a marketplace and said, "Please tell me, I beg you. What were you smuggling?"

"Ah," said the man. "I was smuggling donkeys."

The Goat and the Vine

A goat wandered into a vineyard one day and found vines hanging heavily with the juiciest grapes. The goat trotted over to the nearest stems and began to graze on the tender green shoots.

All of a sudden, it heard a voice. The goat realized with a start that it was the vine speaking!

"Whatever have I done to you for you to hurt me like this?" it sobbed. "Isn't there enough grass for you to feed on?" Before the goat could reply, the vine added, "Even if you eat every leaf and leave me bare, I will still produce wine for the cook to add to the pot – when you are being cooked as a stew."

If you cross somebody, you can be certain they will want to get their own back.

The Man with the Coconuts

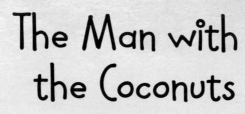

A man and his horse were once heading home after a long day of gathering coconuts. The man asked a boy at the roadside how long it would take him to get to the next town, as he was feeling very tired. The boy saw that the man's horse had a basket on either side, both of which were full of coconuts. "If you go slowly," said the boy, "you will arrive very soon, but if you go fast, it will take you all day."

The man didn't understand, so he hurried his horse. But the coconuts bounced out of the baskets and he had to stop to pick them up. He climbed back into the saddle and hurried his horse to make up for lost time, but the coconuts fell out again. On the third try he let his horse walk slowly. The coconuts stayed in the baskets, and he understood what the boy had meant.

The Swan and the Raven

A raven once caught sight of a swan and couldn't help but feel jealous of the elegant bird's long neck and snow-white feathers. The raven became eaten up with envy — all he could think of was how he too could get the same beautiful plumage!

'Maybe the swan's clean colour comes from the water in which he swims?' the raven wondered. So he went to soak himself in the swan's lakes and pools. But no matter how many times the raven washed, he didn't become even a tiny bit white. Instead, he was bedraggled and hungry, as he couldn't find any food. In the end, he returned to his old home and had to be satisfied with his lot.

You can try to change your behaviour but it won't change what you are.

One's Own Children are always Prettiest

A man once went out into a wood to hunt, and he met a curious little bird – a snipe.

"Dear friend," said the snipe, "don't shoot my children!"

"How shall I know which are your children?" asked the man, "what do they look like?"

"Oh!" said the snipe, proudly, "mine are the prettiest children in all the wood."

"Very well," said the man, "I'll not shoot them – don't be afraid."

But despite his promise, the man came back with a whole string of young snipe in his hand, which he had just shot.

"Oh no!" said the snipe, "why did you shoot my children after you said you would not harm them?"

"What, are these your children!" said the man, "Why, you said they were the prettiest in all of the wood. I shot the ugliest I could find!"

"Don't you know that everyone thinks their own children are the prettiest in the world?" said the snipe very sadly.

The Snail and the Butterfly

A snail once thought to itself, 'I wish I was a butterfly', as it watched a beautiful peacock butterfly flitting by. The snail slid slowly across the grass, looking for tender shoots to eat, and envied the butterfly's delicately painted wings.

Just as the snail reached a tall plant, the skies darkened and huge drops of rain began to fall heavily. The poor butterfly darted under the plant and hung there shivering and terrified.

"If the rain hits my wings, it will brush my paint off and damage them," it said. "If only I could be somewhere safe and dry."

"I wish I could help you," said the snail kindly, "But I carry my house with me and it is only big enough for one."

And as the snail tucked itself snugly inside its home, it felt much better.

POST

The Legend of the Christmas Rose

A robber woman lived deep in the forest with her five wild children. When she needed more food than they could catch themselves, she begged from the townsfolk, who feared her and would not let her live among them.

One day, the robber woman promised to show the townsfolk a magic garden if they would forgive her wild ways. They agreed, and at midnight she took them to the forest. All was dark, but then a beautiful garden appeared, with many flowers blooming together, their scent heavy in the air.

The townspeople cried that it was bad magic, and the garden faded from their sight. Only a single white root remained. This was gathered by a small boy. The townspeople planted it and on Christmas Eve it blossomed. It had silver leaves and flowers, and was the first Christmas rose.

The Snow Queen

Long ago, a wicked sprite made a magic mirror. In it, anything that was good and beautiful had an evil, ugly reflection. One day the mirror was dropped and it smashed into a billion pieces. The wind picked up the dust-like fragments and carried them all over the world.

A little boy called Kay was playing with his friend, Gerda, when suddenly he cried, "Oh, I've got something in my eye!" It was one of the pieces from the magic mirror! Very quickly, Kay became bitter and cruel. He no longer wanted to play with Gerda, and teased her.

One day soon after, Kay saw a large, horse-drawn sleigh glide into the town square. The driver was a woman wrapped up in a white fur cloak. Kay did not know it, but she was the wicked Snow Queen.

"Come and warm up in

my sleigh," she coaxed. Kay climbed in and the Snow Queen kissed his forehead – and with that kiss Kay forgot his home, his family and Gerda.

The Snow Queen cracked the whip and they were soon off to her palace. There Kay stayed with the Snow Queen, having forgotten everything he had once known. How worried everyone was when Kay didn't come back. His parents believed he had drowned, but Gerda decided to look for him and set out to search.

Finally, some wood pigeons told her, "We've seen Kay! He was sitting in the sleigh of the Snow Queen."

"Which way should I go?" cried Gerda.

"Ask our friend, the reindeer."

Gerda found the reindeer at the edge of a forest.

"Do you know where the Snow Queen's palace is?" she asked.

"Of course I do," said the reindeer. "Jump on my back and I will take you."

So off they flew, through the forest and over snowy mountains, until they arrived in Lapland. The reindeer took Gerda right up to the Snow

Queen's glittering ice palace and she found herself in an empty, endless, snowy hall. And there before her sat Kay. He was all alone, for the Snow Queen had flown away on her sleigh.

Gerda ran to Kay in joy, but he just sat there, making patterns in the snow with an icicle.

"Kay!" Gerda whispered. "Don't you remember me?" Still Kay sat, numb and motionless.

Then Gerda began to cry. Her warm tears fell on Kay and melted away the Snow Queen's icy kiss. He slowly began to remember his little friend and he burst into tears too.

"Gerda! Where am I? Why is it so cold?" Kay wept so much that the splinter of mirror in his eye was finally washed out.

"The Snow Queen took you," Gerda explained. "Now come with me — we must escape."

Hand in hand the two ran out of the vast hall and climbed onto the friendly reindeer's back. He flew them through the snowy night, until at last they reached the warmth of their homes.

The Fox and the Snail

One day a fox met a snail and proposed that they should race each other.

"You're on!" said the snail, and set off at once – a little slowly to be sure. But instead of running to the finish line, the fox rested. He thought he had enough time to start in the cool of the evening, so he dozed off. While the fox slept the snail crept into the fox's bushy tail.

When the fox finally started running he was surprised that the snail was nowhere to be seen.

When he reached the end of the race and still couldn't see the snail, he turned around proudly and called out, "Snail, are you coming soon?"

"I'm already here!" answered the snail, for he had climbed down from the fox's tail and crept over the finish line. And the proud fox had to admit that he had lost!

The Prophet Elijah Visits Earth

The Prophet Elijah and a companion were travelling on Earth and needed a place to stay for the night. They came across a cottage and asked the poor couple inside if they could stay. The couple agreed and treated them kindly, feeding them the last of their food. That night, their cow sadly died.

The next night, the Prophet went to ask for shelter at a rich man's house. The man lodged them in his stable and only gave them scraps to eat. The next day the Prophet repaired the man's wall, so his companion asked, "Why did the poor man lose his cow when he treated you well, and the rich man get rewarded for treating you badly?"

The Prophet answered, "The poor man's wife should have died that night, but I asked God to take the cow instead. The rich man would have found a heap of gold hidden in the wall if I hadn't repaired it."

The Wild Boar and the Fox

One fine day, a fox was wandering through a forest, minding his own business, when he came across a wild boar. The boar was hard at work rubbing his white tusks against the bark of a tree to make them fine and sharp.

The fox looked all around. Then he sniffed the air. He could neither see nor smell any hunters that the boar might need to fight off — nor indeed any other dangers.

"My friend, why are you doing that?" asked the fox. "I cannot think of a reason why you are so hard at work preparing your tusks for battle."

"True, comrade," replied the boar. "But the instant my life is in danger I shall need my tusks. There'll be no time to sharpen them then."

Be prepared.

INDEX OF STORIES